TO LOVE AGAIN

Dana Lynn Hites

A KISMET™ Romance

METEOR PUBLISHING CORPORATION
Bensalem, Pennsylvania

KISMET™ is a trademark of Meteor Publishing Corporation

Copyright © 1992 Dana Lynn Hites
Cover Art Copyright © 1992 Laurence Schwinger

First Printing May 1992.

ISBN: 1-56597-007-1

To all the people who believed in me, and especially to Jackie Taylor, my mom—Dee, Lester, George and Gene . . . dreams can come true.

DANA LYNN HITES

Ms. Hites has been writing for thirteen years. Born in Maryland, she wrote **To Love Again** after moving from Hawaii to Washington state. Currently, Ms. Hites shares the home of her cat, Lynx, and is working on her next novel.

ONE

She wasn't the wet T-shirt type.

Cord Wayne leaned back against the cracked red padding that ran the length of the Ramblin' Man Tavern's bar, took a sip from his drink, and continued his survey of the woman from over the top of his glass. He squinted against the haze of cigarette and cigar smoke that thickened the air. The front door opened, sweeping cool night air into the tavern, and he could see her clearly, sitting fifteen feet away at a small round table to his right. She was young, blonde, and just didn't seem the type to enter a wet T-shirt contest.

She didn't fit with the rowdy crowd he'd seen since he entered the small North Carolina tavern with his friend Ronnie. Her almond-shaped eyes, high cheekbones, and the gentle beauty of her fresh scrubbed face set her apart from the other women in the room. But there was something more, something about this particular woman that drew his eyes back to her again and again, albeit against his will.

Cord lowered his glass and absently stroked its slick side with his fingers. His gaze naturally dropped to the

7

woman's body. She might be petite, but she was also voluptuous. She wore a loose-fitting pink T-shirt and jeans that did nothing to emphasize the well-rounded body hidden beneath them. Though jeans and a T-shirt were the standard attire for the night's entertainment, on her they looked different; her shirt wasn't painted on, nor were her jeans a size too small. He found the subtle hints of her shape tantalizing in a way that made him uncomfortable.

His left eyebrow rose as his gaze moved back up her body, following the path of her braid, from her hip, past her abdomen and her full breasts, to stop where it draped over her shoulder. He'd never seen hair that long in his life, and the thick braid promised to unwind into a glorious golden-blond mane.

She's probably the only woman in the room whose hair isn't artistically styled with a super-glue compound, he thought. A picture of her, with her hair free-flowing, flashed through his mind, and he quickly banished the image.

With a shake of his head, Cord let his attention wander across the smoky tavern. His hazel-eyed gaze swept the dance floor to his left. He found Ronnie still dancing, cuddled up to a tall redheaded woman in skintight jeans and a curve-hugging T-shirt. He supposed they called that dancing, but Cord had his doubts it would be considered legal when done, in public, off the dance floor. Ronnie was the reason Cord found himself in the tavern. When given a choice, he preferred his ginger ale with the latest Ludlum novel, not a tavern of hard-working, hard-drinking good ol' boys.

Cord gazed behind the slowly gyrating couple and his attention settled briefly on two men who were moving chairs off a six-inch raised platform. Another man was bringing in two large red plastic buckets; the water in the buckets sloshed and came dangerously close to spilling with each step he took. Cord could only assume the platform would serve as a stage, and had probably done so many times before considering its warped wooden surface.

With the exception of tonight's event, a regular one that apparently needed no advertisement, this tavern was no different from the other ones Ronnie had dragged him into in the past year, all in the name of making Cord have a little "fun." Ronnie might like the smoky, noisy atmosphere of these places, but there was little chance of Cord having fun in one. Cord sighed and took another sip of ginger ale. He tried, unsuccessfully, to block out the sound of the twangy country music playing on the jukebox.

Cord's gaze was drawn back to the woman. He couldn't help questioning why she was in the tavern, if not for the contest. He found himself wondering who she was, and what was wrong that caused a worried frown to wrinkle her brow. A long time ago, he might have walked over and introduced himself; that he even considered the possibility, now, almost scared the hell out of him.

"Did the mechanic come in yet?"

Honey Johnson looked up as her friend, Sally, joined her at the small round table.

"No," Honey replied.

Sally reached over and swiped two of Honey's french fries. With a sigh, Honey pushed the basket of fries into the middle of the table.

"But he promised to have the tire fixed by the time we finished eating."

"I know, but he hasn't shown up yet. Maybe it won't be much longer," Honey said in her soft, unhurried drawl. Reaching up, she flicked her long braid over her shoulder and leaned back against the scarred wooden surface of her rail-backed chair.

"Well . . ." Sally began, reaching up to tuck a curly

brown strand of hair behind her ear. "I, for one, feel better now that I've eaten. My poor stomach was on the verge of rebellion."

"Hmm," Honey sighed. Reaching out, she ran one of her fingers through the wet circles her glass of cola had left on the chipped Formica tabletop.

Sally's blue eyes darkened in sympathy. Instead of reaching for another french fry, she laid her hand over Honey's restless one.

"Don't worry. Everything's going to be great, you'll see. The show will be a hit this year and everyone'll drive you crazy with bookings for next year."

Honey's dark-brown eyes met Sally's. She knew the forced smile she offered didn't fool her friend, but she smiled nonetheless. Sally had spent most of this disappointing day trying to cheer her up. It was a shame she couldn't convince Sally the effort was wasted.

"Yeah, maybe you're right, Sal. After tomorrow we'll know for sure."

"He's coming tomorrow?" Sally's eyes rounded in surprise and her short, curly hair practically quivered in excitement.

"He's supposed to, but . . ." Honey shrugged. With the way her luck was running lately, she didn't want to say for sure.

At a shout and sudden roar from the mostly male crowd, both women turned toward the sound. Honey saw at least thirty or so men pushing toward the small stage against the far wall to her right, but she couldn't see anything more. The jukebox, playing a rousing Waylon Jennings song, went silent. A spotlight came on, and she heard the excited announcement that the show was about to begin.

"A band?" Sally questioned as the men chuckled and started elbowing each other.

"If it is, it must be a popular group."

Not interested in whatever the entertainment was, Honey turned away and looked up at the clock over the bar that advertised a well-known brand of beer. Where was that mechanic? He said thirty minutes to fix her blown tire. It had been over an hour already. Why, oh why, did it have to blow out today of all days? She'd just had a flat last week and hadn't even bothered to get the tire repaired yet. It was sitting in the back of the van, still flat as a pancake. Then, to have another one blow out today, on the drive home, was too much.

Before she could turn to Sally and suggest they go back to the service station, Honey found her wandering attention captured by a man standing at the bar. She'd hate to admit it was the beautiful washboard stomach and broad muscular chest that she first noticed, but how could she pass up a second look at such perfection? It seemed a shame to cover that physique with anything, even if it was a form-fitting light green T-shirt.

Her eyes lingered on the man, noting the way his worn jeans jacket made his shoulders look even broader. She practically sighed. Expecting to be disappointed, Honey looked up and found *him* watching *her*.

He had the most gentle eyes she'd ever seen on a man. They were compelling, hypnotizing, and he seemed startled to find her watching him. The tavern, the growing noise of the crowd, all faded into oblivion. She stared in bemusement, noting the wavy darkness of his hair, the strength of his jawline, and the masculine beauty of his face. But it was his eyes she couldn't break away from. All the secrets of life seemed contained in those dark-fringed eyes of his. And then, he smiled at her. He had such a beautiful, gentle, sexy smile. Her breath caught. Her heart stopped, then kicked into overdrive. Helplessly, Honey smiled back.

"Honey!" Sally's voice ripped through the magic.

"What?" Honey almost snapped at Sally. Since she hadn't turned away from the stranger, she missed Sally's look of startled surprise.

"We've got to get out of here . . ." Sally began.

Honey shook her head. "No."

"Honey, what's wrong with you? Didn't you hear me? We've got to leave."

The worried tone of Sally's voice finally reached Honey. Reluctantly, she turned back to her friend.

"What's wrong, Sal?"

"They're having a wet T-shirt contest tonight," she returned in a hushed whisper. "And some of the men are starting to look at you funny. They might try to force you up on stage." Sally looked around nervously. Then she reached over to pull at Honey's arm, urging her to move as she started to rise.

"A wet . . . ? Oh, come on, Sally! Why don't you just calm down and relax. You're getting worried over nothing." Honey shook her head and smiled. Sally abruptly sat back down, and her mouth opened in silent denial. Once more she looked around. Honey took her cue from Sally and, intending to humor her, she looked up over Sally's shoulder. She met the leering, assessing stare of a burly older man. Quickly she lowered her troubled gaze to the table. What if Sally was right for a change? What if her worry was justified? Honey thought.

"Uh, why don't we head over to the service station. The mechanic should be done by now," Honey suggested, her casual tone masking her own growing nervousness. She stood when Sally nodded in wholehearted agreement.

As she led the way to the door, Honey heard a loud splash from the stage area and the resulting roar of male approval. She started to feel more assessing male glances from the men between her and the exit. When had the door gotten so far away?

Honey felt a vise clamp down on her upper arm, and she was pulled to an abrupt halt.

"You're heading the wrong way sweetie," a slurred voice drawled from somewhere above her.

"Let me go," Honey demanded.

She looked around and up, a long way up. Next to her five foot nothing, the man had to be six five, at least. He wasn't just large, he was mammoth. The dark blue T-shirt he wore strained to cover the huge mound of his stomach, and failed in the attempt. A pale white strip of skin showed above his low-hanging jeans. The smell of stale beer swamped her, and without being told, she knew she was in trouble.

She tried to pull away, but his ham-size fist wouldn't release her arm. She'd have bruises tomorrow, she knew it.

"I said . . ." she began again, trying to reason with him this time.

The mammoth wasn't listening. He turned away and pulled her along behind him. She found it a struggle just to stay upright. She had no doubt he'd drag her along if she fell, probably by her hair.

Honey heard Sally's outraged cry and looked back. She caught a brief glimpse of her before she was blocked from view by the same men who parted easily to allow the mammoth to pass.

"Let me go," Honey demanded breathlessly.

Once again, he didn't listen. She was briefly airborne as he lifted her onto the stage. Behind her, men were laughing and calling encouragement, and she found herself facing six angry women. They weren't any too happy to have her on the stage, and she wasn't any too pleased at being there herself.

Honey quickly turned away, only to be blinded by the spotlight. She shielded her eyes, trying to adjust to the bright light, but it got worse. Men were everywhere, and she felt like they were all leering at her.

"Hey, Lenny, she looks awful tiny to me," a man yelled from the back. Several men snickered in the front row.

Burning anger quickly overcame her fear. How dare they make her a part of this. Enough was enough. She was leaving. She stepped forward, intending to get off the stage and take apart any man who tried to stop her.

The shocking, ice-cold water hit her and stole her breath. She gasped and saw red. The mammoth, Lenny, stood in front of her, laughing, a red bucket dangling loosely from his beefy hand.

"She don't look so tiny now," he called out. Then, he bent over to guffaw in amusement.

Honey didn't think beyond the enraged haze that clouded her vision. She reached down, grabbed the bucket from his loose grip, and swung straight up. With a loud thunk, the bucket clipped him under the chin. The mammoth jerked up and stumbled back, more in surprise than pain. He fell into the half-dozen men standing behind him. En masse, they landed on one of the small tables beside the stage. The table quivered for a moment under their combined weight, then crashed to the floor.

Honey jumped from the stage and dropped the bucket to push at the men who still blocked her path. They moved, slowly, seeming too dumbfounded to do much else. She made her way forward, unaware of the growing shuffling and murmurs behind her.

Halfway across the room, she began to shiver with cold. She stopped and looked down to see her light-purple lace bra showing clearly through the wet material of her pink T-shirt. Her nipples were hard from the cold. Red swept her cheeks and she quickly folded her arms over her breasts. She looked up to find the exit and saw only a wide circle of men closing in on her. She felt trapped, and reaction began to sink in.

"Come on, I'll get you out of here," a deep, husky-velvet male voice said. A jeans jacket enveloped her and a male arm draped over her shoulders, urging her forward.

Automatically, Honey stiffened. Then, she looked up. It was the stranger from the bar, only now, his gentle eyes were filled with concern.

Honey allowed him to guide her, and felt her apprehension fading. She didn't know why she instinctively trusted him, but she did.

They started moving across the room, and an enraged bellow sounded from behind them. Honey didn't need to look to know it was the drunken mammoth.

"Where is she?" The mammoth's bellow echoed through the tavern.

The stranger glanced back then increased his pace, tightening his hold on her. Strident female voices were yelling to disqualify "the uppity blonde." Men were stumbling away from the mammoth, who still lay on the floor, yelling for the blonde and struggling to rise.

Honey and her rescuer broke through the last handful of men and saw Sally, her blue eyes bright with anxiety. Sally took aim at the stranger's head and raised her purse.

"No!" Honey cried.

Sally froze.

"Thanks." The man chuckled, looking down into Honey's dark-brown eyes.

The stranger looked over his shoulder. The mammoth was on his feet and getting closer. He turned back to Honey and pushed her away from him, toward the door. "Go on."

Honey hesitated, surprised he wasn't following her. When she looked back, she saw the mammoth.

"Get out of here. Now!" The stranger spun away to

face the mammoth and Sally pulled Honey through the exit. Before the door closed behind her, Honey heard the unmistakable sound of a fist meeting flesh and winced.

"We can't just leave him," Honey protested as Sally pulled her across the deserted street to the town's lone service station.

"When I couldn't help you, I called the sheriff. Hear that siren? He'll be okay. Now, let's go, or do you want to be a North Carolina headline tomorrow morning, 'Owner of Johnson Airshow in wet T-shirt brawl'?"

Honey shuddered at the thought. She couldn't afford that kind of publicity. She was in enough trouble as it was, and walking a thin line until she could get an investor. There would be no hope of Cord Wayne buying into her airshow if he found out about tonight's fiasco. The bad publicity alone could finish off her show, to say nothing of ruining her last chance at saving it.

The mechanic was pulling Honey's dark-blue van out of the garage as they arrived. After paying the bill, Honey and Sally climbed in and pulled away. In her rearview mirror, she saw the lone sheriff's car arrive and people pouring out of the tavern.

Regret tugged at her. She didn't even know his name.

Cord smiled, rubbed his sore knuckles, and looked down at the unconscious mammoth. It was nice to know he hadn't lost his touch, even if it had been a while since he'd been in a fist fight. All around him, the tavern crowd was fighting with the same enjoyment they'd shown at the onset of the contest. Women screeched, men overturned tables, and an airborne bottle caused Cord to duck. The bottle shattered against the wooden door next to him. He turned to view the remains of the bottle that had almost reparted his hair and felt someone grab his shoulder. Instantly, he spun to face the new threat, his fist raised, arm cocked to deliver another jaw-crunching blow.

"Hey!" his friend Ronnie cried as he instinctively ducked.

"Sorry," Cord returned and let his arm fall back to his side.

"Some fun, huh?" Ronnie asked with a grin, reaching up to push a thick lock of black hair off his forehead. Cord gave the younger man an exasperated frown and shook his head.

"The RV's out back. Let's get the hell out of here." Cord led the way, moving toward the back door.

Two burly young men stepped away from the bar and blocked Cord's path. Almost identical grins of anticipation split their faces as they waited for him to reach them. Splintering wood and a pained groan sounded behind Cord. One of the young men sprang for Cord, and Cord slipped under his outstretched arms, moving quickly out of reach. The man ran into Ronnie, who, quick as a cat, rolled with the grab and tossed the man over his head before rolling back up to his feet again. A cocky, reckless grin curved Ronnie's lips.

"Next," he called.

Cord shot a disgusted look at Ronnie before he moved toward the exit and the man still blocking his path. The young man seemed frozen in place. He looked from his fallen buddy, to Ronnie, and then to Cord. Holding up both his hands, he moved away, backing up until he ran into the door to the ladies' room. Without bothering to look at the door, he pushed it open and slipped inside.

Cord and Ronnie moved quickly, exiting the tavern as a scream and crash came from the bathroom and two uniformed officers pushed open the front door.

After they were safely in the large RV and pulling away

from the rapidly emptying building, both men heaved a sigh of relief.

"You mind tellin' me what that was all about?" Ronnie asked. From his position on the worn passenger chair, Cord merely shook his head. He still couldn't believe how much trouble one woman had managed to cause, all within the space of fifteen minutes.

"Did it have something to do with the half-pint pixie who beaned the giant? I lost track of her once she pushed into the crowd. Next thing I know, all hell's breaking loose."

"She didn't want to be part of the entertainment," Cord replied. Lord, that was an understatement. He could still remember the exact instant when he'd figured out something was *very* wrong.

"I think that was pretty plain when she blasted the drunk with the bucket. But did you get a look at her? Now that kind of bod would have won hands down. 'Course, the bra wasn't exactly fair, but . . .''

"Ronnie, leave it," Cord snapped. Seeing the shocked surprise widen Ronnie's dark-blue eyes, Cord almost groaned. What was wrong with him?

"Damn," he muttered to himself. "I'm sorry, Ronnie, I don't know what's gotten into me," he said by way of apology, and it was true. He didn't know what was wrong, he only knew he didn't want Ronnie making disparaging remarks about the woman.

"Yeah, well, it's okay." Ronnie shrugged. He adjusted the radio until he found the rock music he enjoyed.

"We headin' for the Johnson Airshow, like your dad asked?" Ronnie questioned casually, almost too casually.

Cord's sharp gaze sliced through the semidarkness and fastened on Ronnie's profile. He knew Ronnie well enough to distrust that oh-so-casual tone.

"You know I turned that assignment down. I'm not

interested in any business that deals with airplanes.'' His sharp reply permitted no arguments.

''I just figured since we were so close and all.''

''Well, you figured wrong. We are not stopping at any airshow. We're going to Florida, and we may just take in the sights and have a real spring break like everyone else. For tonight, just find us a campground as far away from the Ramblin' Man Tavern as you can get. I've had enough excitement and 'fun' for one day.''

''Yeah, sure,'' Ronnie returned with a shrug.

After a moment, Cord rose and headed back to his bedroom. Automatically, he adjusted his stride to the rocking movement of the motor home. As he stripped off his T-shirt and jeans, he couldn't help thinking of the woman he'd given his jacket to. There was no way he'd ever see her again, which was probably for the best. She made him feel things he hadn't felt in over a year, things he had never thought to feel again. He wanted nothing to do with her, absolutely nothing.

TWO

The sun could be rude. Cord groaned and finally gave up. Last night, he'd forgotten to close the blinds on his bedroom windows. Now, he was paying the price. His bed was bathed in light, and he knew he might as well get up.

Cord stumbled out of bed and headed for the bathroom. When he emerged, he opted for a hot shower at the camp facilities over a cold one in the RV. He pulled on a pair of jeans, grabbed a change of clothes, bar of soap, and a towel before heading out the door.

It took half a dozen steps before he came up short. Where were the showers? Where were the other campers? For that matter, where was the campground?

Where the devil was he?

Looking around, squinting against the bright early-morning sunlight, Cord found nothing but barren sand and sea oats. However, the surface where he stood was pavement, very hot pavement.

"Damn," Cord exclaimed as his bare feet complained. He jumped back into the shade of the RV and almost sighed in relief.

From this vantage point, he could see the pavement was more like a . . . runway. He was going to kill Ronnie.

Cord looked to the left and saw a large brown hangar and several brightly colored planes, but it was the woman heading toward him that made him do a double take. She looked a lot like the woman from the tavern. In fact, she looked exactly like the woman from the tavern, right down to the beautiful golden-blond braid. But this morning, she was wearing a dirt-streaked, body-molding khaki coverall.

He shook his head in disbelief. Only thirty-one and he was losing his mind. Ronnie's craziness had finally gotten to him. He wouldn't be surprised to see Rod Serling and hear weird music any minute now.

"Hello," the vision called, still some distance away.

Cord didn't attempt to answer, he lowered his head in the hopes all this would go away. He knew he had to be in the middle of some crazy dream. Life just didn't work this way.

Honey Johnson approached the beat-up Pace Arrow with a certain amount of trepidation. The man standing in the shade of the motor home hadn't even bothered to answer her greeting, and the RV didn't have a lot to recommend it. It looked as though whoever drove it had terrible depth perception. Every corner had been crunched at least once. This couldn't be Cordell Wayne, of the Wayne and Cray Air Associates in Maryland.

When she stepped into the shade of the motor home, and the man looked up, she gasped in recognition. Her hand went to the dusty aluminum on the side of the RV to steady herself. It couldn't be, but it was. The stranger from the tavern was standing on her runway, not five feet from her.

"Good heavens!"

"I could think of a better way to put it," he said as he finally faced her.

His deep, husky voice was enough to melt her senses. She'd dreamed about that voice last night, and the sexy stranger from the tavern. It was too much to have the flesh-and-blood man standing on her runway.

"You're the man from the tavern," she said, but it almost sounded like an accusation.

"Yes." He sighed in acceptance.

Honey lost any ability she might have had to say more when she looked down and realized he was bare from neck to waist. And what a beautiful bareness it was, well muscled and covered with dark curling hair that arrowed down to the waistband of his unsnapped jeans.

Honey lowered her eyes and felt her cheeks heating with a blush. She was thankful he couldn't read her thoughts. Two years a widow and suddenly she was becoming a sex maniac. What was wrong with her? When she looked up, she knew what was wrong. She'd never been faced with such blatant masculinity in all her twenty-five years.

"Look . . ." he began, stepping closer and then pausing when she quickly looked up and her startled eyes met his.

"I . . ." Honey began and stammered to silence.

Neither one seemed capable of saying more. She just stared, discovering the little things she'd missed the night before. She saw his eyes were hazel and his hair was dark brown and had a tendency to curl. He stood barely a head taller than her own five foot nothing, but he'd seemed much taller last night, in the tavern.

Cord found, in full daylight, she was still a beauty. Her almond-shaped eyes of melting chocolate were all the more striking with her blond hair. She was tiny, and yet round and shapely all the same. She was trouble.

"What is it with you two? I've heard people talk better on game shows," Ronnie said as he stepped into the doorway, standing behind the closed screen door.

Honey and Cord jumped in surprise and turned to face the younger man. Ronnie threw open the screen and a lopsided grin curved his lips.

"Hey, you're the pixie with the big . . ."

"Ronnie!"

"Uh, you're the girl from last night."

"Yes . . ." Honey began hesitantly. Guilt assailed her when she saw the bruise high on the younger man's cheek. She could only assume he had been in the tavern, though he seemed too young to drink, much less frequent such a place.

"You missed a hell of a fight, should have stuck around," Ronnie drawled.

"Fight?" Honey replied, her eyes rounding. He *had* been there, and there'd been a fight, a fight she'd caused.

"Yeah. Glass and fists were flying. We almost got our heads bashed, and . . ." Ronnie continued with undaunted enthusiasm, ignoring Cord's silencing frown.

"Oh, Lord," Honey cried and slumped back against the RV.

"Hey . . ." Ronnie began as he jumped down from the doorway and stopped a few feet from Honey.

"Shut up, Ronnie, or so help me I'm going to knock some sense into that thick head of yours," Cord snapped. He tossed his things into the doorway of the RV and moved to Honey's side. Her head was bowed, her eyes closed, and her shoulders were slumped.

"Are you okay?" Cord asked softly.

"Were you hurt?" Honey's question was soft, but he heard it.

"No. We're fine. My friend, Ronnie, just has a strange sense of humor."

Honey's head came up and her eyes opened. Her gaze touched Ronnie's bruised cheek.

"But the bruise?" she questioned, obviously distressed.

"Now look what you've done," Cord said over his shoulder to Ronnie. "Will you tell this woman you're okay?"

Ronnie was watching Honey with the strangest look on his face. He stepped up to Cord's side and met her concerned eyes. Slowly, a smile curved his lips. Cord had never seen such a tender expression, however brief, soften Ronnie's features. He looked younger, more innocent than the twenty-one years he claimed.

"I'm fine, half-pint," Ronnie said, his voice low and reassuring.

"But you're hurt."

"Hell, I've been hurt worse and not had as much fun," he returned.

Honey seemed to relax, but she didn't leave the support of the RV.

"Do you want to come inside?" Cord asked.

"No. I'm fine, and if I go inside, my crew will probably storm your RV. I had a fight when I left, alone, to see what you were doing on my runway," she replied with a smile.

"*Your* runway?" Cord questioned in a strange, stilted voice.

"Yes." She heard Ronnie's low whistle and frowned.

"*You're* Ms. Johnson, of the Johnson Airshow?" Cord asked.

"Yesss," Honey drawled softly. As the light of realization dawned, horror replaced her puzzlement.

"*You're* Cord Wayne?" she asked, half fearfully.

"Yes."

"Dayum!" Honey cried, and quickly clapped her hand over her mouth.

Both men rocked back on their heels, startled by her reaction.

"I'm sorry. I didn't mean to . . ." Honey began,

clearly mortified at the thought she might have offended them in addition to involving them in a barroom brawl.

One look at Honey and Ronnie started to chuckle. Soon, he was laughing so hard he stumbled over to lean against the RV.

Cord didn't bother to look down at her. His jaw clenched and his hands flexed and fisted at his sides. He had no intention of staying here any longer than it took to tell her he was leaving. The night before, he'd made it plain to Ronnie that he wasn't interested in an airshow. He hadn't changed his mind in the few hours since. Cord turned to face Ronnie, ready to blast him with the heat of his anger. Ronnie was too busy laughing to care. Spinning back to face Honey, Cord looked down and saw her distress.

"Oh, Lord," Honey muttered as she pushed away from the RV and started pacing.

"Is it really that bad?" Cord asked, forgetting his anger in the face of her obvious distress.

"Yes," she sighed. Honey stopped and looked up at him. She frowned, turned away, and resumed her pacing. Nothing had gone right for her lately, she couldn't imagine why she'd thought her meeting with Cord Wayne would be any different. With another sigh, she shook her head.

"I'd like to start this week again."

"The week's almost over, why start it again?" he replied reasonably.

"Oh. Well, you don't know what kind of week it's been. Everything has gone wrong. One of my planes has a mysterious oil leak. The lead I had on a cheap hot air balloon rig turned out to be just that, hot air. And to top it off, the one man who can help my show turns out to be the same man who saw me institute a brawl in the middle of a wet T-shirt contest. How can it get much worse?" she asked, and her troubled brown eyes met his.

He melted. There was no other word for it. She looked

up at him and he couldn't bring himself to make it even worse. How could he tell her he had no intention of staying and looking over her show?

"Why were you at the tavern last night?" he asked instead.

"A blown tire. We made it to the service station across the street from the tavern, and we were starving. The tavern was the only other place open, so we went in to eat and wait. The rest you know. It was not my finest hour."

"Oh, I don't know about that, you sure took out that giant. By the way, my name's Ronnie Hunter, since Cord's forgotten his manners and hasn't bothered to introduce me," Ronnie drawled from his position by the RV.

"Nice to meet you," she replied automatically as she looked over at him, "and please don't remind me of last night."

"Ronnie, go make coffee or something," Cord ordered.

With a shrug, Ronnie disappeared into the RV and shut the screen door after him. Cord turned back to Honey only to find her watching him intently.

"I guess it's kind of silly to ask you for a second chance, but I'd like one. Will you come to . . . uh . . . will you stop by my house and we can talk? I'd like a little time to let my people know you're actually here so we can get cleaned up and all," Honey said.

Suddenly, she seemed nervous, and Cord couldn't blame her. He wanted to suggest they meet in her office, but thought better of it. She had had enough thrown at her for now.

"When and where?" he replied instead.

She smiled at him, and the sun seemed to grow brighter. She quickly gave him directions to her beach house in Sequoyah, north of Kitty Hawk, said good-bye, and headed back to the large dark brown hangar with a spring in her step.

Cord looked up and found the banner proclaiming JOHNSON AIR SHOW—VISITORS WELCOME in bold red letters over the hangar doors. If they were all met by Ms. Johnson, he had no doubt they were indeed welcome. There was a warmth that seemed to radiate out of her. He'd noticed it when she looked at him the night before, and then again, today. What the devil was he going to do now?

A scowl pulled Cord's brows together as he reached for the screen door. There was one thing he could take care of, a certain interfering friend who couldn't follow the simplest of directions.

"Ronnie . . ."

The peal of the doorbell rent the silence of Honey's beach house. She spun away from the sliding glass doors, quickly made one final check of her immaculate living room, and headed for the front door.

"Well, at least this is better than my office," she muttered to herself.

She stopped before she opened the door and looked through the peephole. Seeing Cord, she stepped back and ran her sweaty palms down the legs of her faded blue jeans. A quick tug at the hem of her green cotton shirt, a swipe at the wispy hairs that had escaped her braid, a deep breath, and she was ready. With a smile of greeting, Honey opened the door to Cordell Wayne, her last hope.

"Hello. Did you have any trouble finding my place?" she asked, trying to hide her nervousness.

"No, and the drive along the beach was relaxing." Cord's tone was overly polite, but she didn't notice. Warily, he entered.

Ronnie bounded up the stairs and Honey looked up, offering him a welcoming smile as she closed the door behind him.

"Can I get either of you something to drink?" she questioned as she moved back into the living room.

"We'll take ginger ale if you have any," Cord replied before Ronnie could say anything.

"I'll be right back. Please feel free to make yourselves comfortable." Honey padded across the large open room and disappeared behind a white swinging door.

Cord stood without moving in the center of the living room. He had that eerie feeling again, a feeling of unreality. *What's wrong with this picture?* kept running through his mind.

It wasn't that the small, older house was without charm. What it lacked was personality. It sat on a sloping sandy hill on the Outer Banks, and the wall of thick glass, facing the ocean, was probably all that made the place bearable. There were no pictures, no knickknacks other than seashells, nothing that marked this as a home. Even the few scattered plants looked fake. He couldn't help but shudder at the thought of fake plants invading anyone's home.

"Kind of . . ." Cord began. The word "sterile" came to mind.

"Yeah," Ronnie replied, looking around with equal curiosity.

"Here you go," Honey said as she came back through the swinging door with a tray of iced drinks.

"Please, sit down so we can talk," she requested, afraid she hadn't put them at ease when she saw them still standing where she'd left them. She headed for the blue flower-patterned couch and placed the tray on the rattan-and-glass coffee table. She sat down on the plush blue-gray chair near the stone fireplace and hoped they would take the hint. It was unnerving to have them towering over her.

Ronnie sprawled onto the couch and Cord took the chair facing her. Cord reached for a glass, seemed to think better of it, and ended up just hanging his linked hands between his jean-clad knees. The blue-and-white striped sports shirt he wore pulled taut over his shoulders, and he seemed to be looking for a way to start.

"Is something wrong?" she asked, her voice soft. She hadn't expected him to be uncomfortable because of their first meeting, but maybe he was. It had been unconventional to say the least.

With a sigh, Cord looked up and saw the gentle question in her eyes.

"I've been trying to think of how to say this since we talked this morning, and well, there just isn't an easy way," he began.

Already, she didn't like the sound of this. Unconsciously, her hands tightened around the slick surface of her glass.

"Ms. Johnson . . ."

"Honey, please."

"What?"

"Honey. It's my name," she replied, puzzled by his shocked look.

"Oh, uh, right. Well . . . Honey . . . What I need to tell you is, we won't be staying." Cord almost sighed in relief to have it out in the open. He had thought about it all morning, and the more he thought, the more he realized he couldn't have her raising her hopes unnecessarily.

Honey froze and just stared at him. So many thoughts ran through her mind, thoughts of the plans she'd made for the airshow, thoughts of the people who depended on her. The airshow was her life, it was all she had, and without Cord Wayne, she was going to lose it.

"Ms. John— Honey, did you hear me?" Cord asked, concerned because of her continued silence.

"I . . ." she had to try again when her voice broke. "I heard," she finally managed to whisper. "Excuse me."

Cord watched her rise with a poise and dignity many

would envy. She moved into the kitchen, and when the door closed behind her, he heard a loud crash and the sound of splintering glass.

Cord and Ronnie looked at each other. Then, Cord jumped up and was at the kitchen door before Ronnie could move.

Cord found her standing in the middle of the bright antiseptic room. The glass lay in a shattered mess on the floor, by the sink near where she stood. She glanced up as Cord entered, then quickly turned away, but not before he saw the silent tears running down her cheeks. She didn't appear hurt, at least not by the broken glass, but her hands were clenched at her sides and her entire body was rigid.

He couldn't stand it. Without thinking, he pulled her around, into the protective circle of his arms and rocked her, holding her close to his chest. He was a jerk.

"I . . . I'm sorry. I didn't mean to . . ." Honey began, trying to push away from him.

"Hush. Just hold still. I wish I could make this easier. I wish I could help," Cord murmured soothingly.

Honey didn't respond. She let her body relax against him. It felt so good to be held again, so good to be held by *him*. She felt safe, as she had the night before.

"You can't help, and I should be ashamed for hanging on you this way," she finally said. But still, she didn't move away.

"That's okay. Hang on as long as you need to. We're hardly strangers," Cord replied, and it was true. He felt as if he'd known her for years. It was enough to make him want to run for the hills, but he couldn't do that to her. He couldn't leave her hurting.

"We *are* strangers. I . . . I wanted to thank you for last night. You helped me, and I appreciated it."

"Forget last night. I have." A lie, but it seemed to be a necessary one if the strain in her voice was anything to go by. In truth, the sight of her in a wet T-shirt was not one he wanted to erase from his mind, ever.

"How can I forget. I made a fool of myself and ruined any chance of getting your help." Honey pushed away from the comfort of his embrace. She was enjoying it too much. Her body, until now, had never betrayed her. Honey hugged herself, covering her breasts to hide her body's reaction to him. Leaning back against the pale-pink counter, she faced him.

Cord shoved his hands into the front pockets of his jeans and rocked back on his heels.

"That's not why," he stated.

Honey's brow furrowed with her silent question, and Cord sighed.

"Honey, I don't buy into businesses dealing with planes."

"But . . . I don't understand. You designed and tested planes up North, and your business . . ." she began in confusion.

"That was a while back. I don't choose to . . . I mean I'm not interested in . . . Oh, hell." Cord lifted his right hand and rubbed the back of his neck. His head lowered, and he stared at the beige-and-white linoleum tile on the kitchen floor.

"Why wasn't I told, Cord?" she asked softly.

Cord almost flinched at the sound of his name. It was the first time she'd used it, and the hurt and confusion in her voice made him feel terribly selfish. It wasn't her fault, none of it was her fault.

"I don't know why you weren't told, Honey," Cord said as he looked up, letting his hand drop back to his side. He knew why she wasn't told. He'd been set up. He also knew, as soon as he faced her and saw her bewildered, beautiful face, that he couldn't walk away as he'd planned.

"I don't understand."

Though it went against every instinct he possessed, he

knew he had to look over the show. However, his one consoling thought was that once he discharged that responsibility, he could leave, as fast as possible. And he would leave. He had to.

"Listen, I'll stay long enough to look over your show, evaluate your business, and make a decision based on my findings. I won't offer you any promises."

"I don't need any," Honey replied earnestly. A chance was all she'd wanted, all she'd dreamed of and prayed for for weeks. He was the last hope she had of making her dream a reality. That he was willing to give her that chance was almost too good to be true.

"Uh, yes . . . well . . ." Cord shifted uncomfortably. The absolute trust and hope in her eyes made him all too aware of his own intentions.

"What gives?" Ronnie called as he pushed open the swinging door.

Cord turned to Ronnie in relief. He knew he had to get away from Honey Johnson before he promised her anything and everything she wanted. She had the most disturbing effect on him and he didn't like it. He didn't like it one bit.

"Nothing," Cord replied. "Are you ready to go?"

"Go?" Ronnie asked carefully.

"Yes. We'll park the RV by the hangar and camp there," Cord began as he led the way out of the kitchen and toward the front door. Ronnie followed him, a puzzled look on his face, and Honey padded silently along behind the two men.

"You know, if you like, you could park in the drive. I could take you in to the hangar and you'd be near the ocean, a shower, and home cooking." Why had she offered that? Cord Wayne already disturbed her more than was safe for her peace of mind, and here she'd gone and practically invited him to move in with her.

"All right!"

"Ronnie," Cord growled.

"Well, I'm tired of cold showers and your cooking." Ronnie shrugged.

"What does he cook?" Honey questioned curiously.

Solemnly, Ronnie met her eyes. "TV dinners."

"TV . . . ?" Staring at the polished wood of the floor, Honey couldn't bring herself to look up.

"What's *wrong* with TV dinners?"

"Noth-nothing, Cord," she replied dutifully. Secretly, she thought his defensiveness rather sweet.

"I'm not sure what will work out best," Cord said, effectively cutting off any further comment on his culinary skills. "Perhaps we can stay the night in your drive and decide tomorrow," Cord offered, and practically bit his tongue after the words left his mouth. He knew better than anyone that staying in the same general vicinity as this woman was one dangerous proposition.

"Fine. Oh, Cord, you may need this." Honey reached behind the door and pulled his jeans jacket off the coat rack. Cord took the jacket with a murmured "Thanks."

"I'll see you later then?"

"Sure. Come on, Ronnie." Cord practically pushed Ronnie out the door in front of him. Without another word, Cord left the beach house, his jacket slung over his arm, and almost sighed in relief as he breathed in the salty sea air. He needed the fresh air just to clear his head of Honey's clean, womanly scent. He only wished it were that easy to erase the image of the woman from his mind.

Pop!

"I thought I told you to get rid of that gum?" Cord growled.

"I did. When we saw the half-pint pixie, I didn't chew any."

"Well get rid of it again, and her name's Honey."

"Sure." Pop!

"At least stop popping the stuff," Cord sighed in defeat. Flopping onto the compact couch, Cord lifted one leg, draped it over the beige cushion back, covered his eyes with his arm, and absently rubbed his abdomen.

"Whatcha gonna do?" Ronnie asked casually. He sat slouched in one of the well-worn dark-brown chairs across from Cord.

"I don't know," Cord replied, too confused to think clearly.

"We stayin' here at the beach house?"

"I don't know."

"You gonna invest in her show?"

"I don't know."

"You gonna hop in the sack with her?"

"I don . . . *What*?" Cord's head turned. His arm dropped back onto the couch, and his eyes opened to glare at the younger man. Ronnie flashed him a lopsided smile in response, revealing several chipped white teeth.

"Well, are you?"

"How should I know?"

"You know," Ronnie stated. He sprang up from the chair and ducked a hanging ivy plant as he headed for the kitchen area. He spit his gum into the trash and opened the refrigerator.

"Why do you care all of a sudden? You've been throwing women at me for months now," Cord snapped defensively.

"Yeah, and you haven't taken even one of them."

"So?"

Ronnie grabbed a soda, slammed the refrigerator, and headed back to his chair. He dropped onto the chair, and as he opened his soda, he caught and held Cord's gaze with his own.

"The tension between you two is so thick even I can feel it. But this woman's different. You could hurt her."

"You think I'll *hurt* her?"

"I think you will. You react to her more than any woman I've seen you with in over a year. But, you're still runnin', still mixed up. I think you'll probably hurt her pretty bad."

"How?"

"Take a good guess," Ronnie snapped.

"Who made you her bodyguard?" came Cord's sarcastic reply.

"Nobody. But she's a tiny little thing, small, vulnerable, and defenseless," Ronnie murmured in response.

"And you've always had a thing for small, helpless creatures." There was no sarcasm this time, only acceptance. Cord understood only too well. As a child, he had cared for any animal he found. It was one of the traits he and Ronnie shared.

Cord knew, with Honey, he was fighting his own protective instincts. The longer he stayed, the greater the danger. He couldn't afford to stay. He didn't like the way she made him feel. She walked right through the barriers he'd spent over a year erecting, and he didn't like it.

"Don't worry, we won't be here long enough to hurt her."

With a long-suffering sigh, Ronnie settled back in his chair and draped one of his long legs over the padded chair arm. He gave Cord a disgusted scowl as he replied, "That'll hurt her, too."

Cord looked away. He couldn't allow Ronnie to sway him. He knew what it was to hurt. He'd been hurting for the past year, and he knew staying here, being around Honey Johnson and her air show, was only going to make it worse.

THREE

Standing alone on the beach, Cord tucked his hands into the back pockets of his jeans. Silently, he watched the ocean sweeping in to caress the sandy shore before reluctantly pulling away. Moonlight sparkled and danced on the silvery-dark surface of the cresting waves, hypnotizing in its effect on him. It was peaceful here, so very peaceful. A deserted beach at night was the perfect place to think. He didn't *want* to think.

Cord took a deep breath, and the material of his off-white fisherman's sweater stretched across the broad expanse of his chest. He raised his clasped hands toward the darkened sky and arched his back. Tucking his hands into the front pockets of his jeans, he prowled toward the beckoning water, his bare feet sinking into the coolness of the shifting sand. His thoughts kept returning to the past, to a time when he had everything, and then lost it in a matter of hours.

Cord felt the chilled sea foam lap across his feet, wetting the lower legs of his jeans. It was like having a cold hand from the past reach out to grab him. As the wave receded, the sand shifted under his feet, pulling at him.

Looking down, Cord allowed a deep sigh to escape his lips and his shoulders to hunch forward.

"Why?" The gentle sea breeze carried away the velvet rasp of his voice. Rhythmic waves hid the sound of his impassioned cry for a reason. "Why?"

He knew it was a mistake to stay in one place for too long, and especially to stay here. There was no way he could help but remember, no way he could stop the pain from returning. How could he keep the memories at bay when he was back at an airfield, where it all started?

Walking faster, away from the memories, away from the past, Cord stumbled across a piece of driftwood half buried in the sand. Regaining his balance, he turned to stare at the inky patch of saturated wood, watching the water swirl up, over, and around it before receding back to leave more and more of the darkened wood exposed.

A stumbling block—just like Ms. Honey Johnson. From the moment he made the decision to help her, in the tavern, he knew she was going to be trouble. It seemed ironic that he would meet her again and that she would be the owner of a failing airshow.

How was he supposed to fight her when she didn't even fight back? All she did was look up at him with those liquid eyes of hers and he said things he had no intention of saying. How was he supposed to fight the response of his own body whenever he was around her? He hadn't expected *that* complication, not so soon, especially not now, and not with Honey. She wasn't anything like Gina. Damn!

Looking up, Cord's gaze settled on Honey's beach house. He retraced his steps, veering off to reach the dry ground farther from the water. He dropped down to sit on the sand and leaned forward to rest his elbows on his crossed legs, staring out toward the horizon. The sound of the ocean and the rustling sea oats surrounded him.

He plunged his fingers into the cool sand and lifted a handful to watch it sift through his fingers. Memories of Gina, the first time he saw her, came to torment his mind.

"You okay?"

Shaken from his painful memories, Cord looked up. Ronnie stood three feet away, barefoot, in jeans and a light blue T-shirt that Cord knew read: They Can't Fire Me, Slaves Have To Be Sold! The moonlight, and the glow of lights from a neighbor's beach house, showed Cord Ronnie's tousled black hair and the clear depths of his eyes, eyes filled with concern and a great deal of world-weary wisdom for his age.

"I'm okay," Cord replied softly. He turned his attention back to the shore, a subtle hint which Ronnie totally ignored.

"Yeah, right," Ronnie drawled. Without asking, he moved closer and sat down next to Cord.

"You're going to catch a chill if you stay out here in a T-shirt. It might be spring, but the nights are still cool."

"I'll survive," Ronnie returned, refusing to be put off.

Cord gave up. Instead, he chose to ignore Ronnie's presence. Once again, his thoughts turned to Gina.

"You're remembering Gina, ain't you?"

"Yes," Cord admitted. He wasn't surprised by Ronnie's perceptiveness, it had happened too often in the past. Ronnie was always there when he needed to talk.

"Because of Honey?" Ronnie asked.

"Yes."

"Is it gonna bother you that much to look at the air show?"

Cord arched one brow and looked over at Ronnie in disbelief. Even in the shadows, Ronnie couldn't mistake that look.

"Yeah, that *was* a stupid question. But Cord, she could have died walkin' across the street."

"Ronnie, she didn't die walking across the street. Gina died flying a plane. She died in a storm she never should have flown into, just to be with me. Two damn months before the wedding!" Cord returned, the growling depths of his voice revealing his inner rage and pain.

"Cord, there wasn't anything you could have done," Ronnie began in a much-repeated refrain.

"The hell there wasn't!" Cord cried, pounding his clenched fist into the sand.

She'd been such a beautiful soft-spoken woman, so sweet, so innocent. It hurt just to think of her. She'd also been the daughter of his partner, Antony Cray, and so damn young to die that way. She'd been barely twenty-one, and she'd been the sunshine in his life. It didn't matter that he was nine years older, at least not to her, and eventually, not to him, either. Before her, he'd known only work, and the never-ending drive to succeed and make money.

"Dammit, Cord, there wasn't anything you, or anyone else, could have done," Ronnie began again, breaking into Cord's thoughts. "You know there wasn't. We'd been traveling together for over a year, knew each other five years before that while I worked for you and Antony. Don't you think I'd tell you if I thought you were right?"

"Leave it, Ron," Cord snapped. His gaze pierced through the darkness and pinned Ronnie with his hot anger. "You might have pulled me out of the bottle last year, but that doesn't mean I need you to absolve me of guilt. You can't."

"Cord, I owe . . ."

"You owe me nothing, not one blasted thing. I gave you a job, but you worked hard with the mechanics. You earned your way at the airfield. Remember that. I don't want your gratitude, or your pity."

"You ain't getting either one, you stubborn horse's—"

"Ronnie," Cord warned softly.

"What you *are* getting from me is friendship, same as you give. You left the company, and I wanted to see the sights. That's it."

"Sure," Cord replied. And he knew if he actually believed it, Ronnie probably had a bridge on Florida swampland that was for sale. Cord knew Ronnie's quirky sense of honor. They were friends, yes, but Ronnie believed he owed Cord a debt, and he was going to make sure it was repaid.

"Uh, Cord . . ." Ronnie began again, only this time his voice was oddly hesitant.

Cord knew what was coming.

"If you're going to say you and my father set me up, I already know it." Cord turned to face Ronnie once more, meeting the younger man's eyes, and seeing his uncertainty even in the darkness.

"When you refused to discuss this job with your dad or Antony, they talked to me. They figured it was time, Cord."

"Time by their standards, Ron, not mine," Cord responded with a touch of irritation. He didn't like being pushed.

"They just want you to be happy—and whole again." Ronnie's soft statement was almost lost in the sound of the surf.

Cord sighed. "I know. I haven't been back in a year. They're worried. But that doesn't mean I'll be able to look at this operation objectively."

Cord knew he had to face his memories, and himself. He knew he had to stop trying to forget, stop running. Perhaps it was time. Yet that didn't make it any easier to accept.

"I think it's time we get some sleep. Morning comes early, and we have a lot to get done," Cord said as he uncrossed his legs and stood, taking a deep breath of the crisp, salty sea air.

Ronnie rose, shivering a little from the chill air, and followed Cord silently. As they neared the motor home, Cord knew he would sleep peacefully tonight. Thanks to Ronnie, he had gotten through the worst of it. Ronnie was family, sometimes more like a brother than a friend. It was not the first time this past year that Ronnie had helped him through a rough night.

Tomorrow, Cord would be back in a hangar, where he hadn't been in over a year. But for now, he'd had enough of memories and the pain they brought.

The next morning, Cord watched the dust motes dancing in the early-morning sunlight that slanted through the window blinds in his small bedroom. He'd been wrong; he hadn't slept well. His problem: the awakening of his body to one petite, sexy blonde. He had no intention of ever being hurt again, but that really didn't answer the problem of Honey Johnson and her invasion of his dreams. He had to get away.

Crawling out of bed, Cord pulled on his jeans and stumbled into the bathroom before entering the compact kitchen. He poured water and coffee into the battered metal coffeepot, put it on the burner, and adjusted the flame. Taking a few steps, he flung open the aluminum door.

"What the hell!" Ronnie yelled, having been rudely awakened when the door swung around to smack against the side of the motor home.

Tumbling out of the loft bed, Ronnie looked down and pierced Cord with a murderous glare. "You got something against sleeping today?"

Cord's lips twitched in an effort to suppress his satisfied

grin. "How about one of those pancake-and-sausage breakfasts?"

Pushing past Cord, Ronnie crowded his six-foot frame into the bathroom. "No," he snapped, closing the door in Cord's face.

Cord took the bathroom again after Ronnie, brushing his teeth and running a battery-powered razor over the coarse stubble along his jaw and chin. After showering quickly for cleanliness, not pleasure, Cord stepped out of the bathroom refreshed and naked.

Ronnie, now clean, more awake, and in a slightly better frame of mind, glanced up from his morning coffee to pin Cord with bright blue eyes full of rebellion.

"I'm tired of frozen breakfast, lunch, and dinner."

Pulling on snug red briefs and another pair of jeans, Cord shrugged, bending to riffle through one of the drawers in the hall closet.

"So fix it yourself," he mumbled through the folds of the dark green sports shirt he pulled over his head.

"You know I don't cook."

"Yesss," Cord drawled.

"And I'm tired of cold showers. When you getting the hot water thing fixed?"

Cord arched a brow at the younger man. He turned to face him after he poured his own coffee. "When I get time and can find the right part."

For some reason, Ronnie was spoiling for a fight. Unable to guess why, Cord sank onto the bench-seat across the table from him.

"What's wrong with you this morning?"

"You ain't gonna give her a fair shake, are you? I thought about it last night, after we got back here. I know you ain't gonna hang around here much longer."

"What are you talking about?"

Ronnie met Cord's gaze without fear. "You heard me."

"All right, why do you think that?"

Ronnie lifted one shoulder negligently, waiting for Cord to deny it. "You wanna run again."

"I don't want to be here, Ronnie, but I'll listen and observe with an open mind." Cord couldn't pretend with Ronnie, and he didn't try. He *had* been thinking of getting away, as fast as he could. It was the only thought keeping him sane.

"But you're gonna leave just the same. You'll listen, but even if it's good, you ain't staying." Slouching down onto the cushions, Ronnie glared at Cord, daring him to say differently.

Cord sipped his coffee without responding. His mind replayed his thoughts of the day before, and this morning. That was what he planned, to take a quick look then leave. Sighing, he relented.

"I promise to give her a fair hearing, and I promise to invest if it's a sound proposition. Is that good enough?" Cord asked.

"Yeah. I guess so."

Cord rose and dumped the rest of his coffee down the drain. "I'm going for a walk."

Shrugging, Ronnie settled back against the wall and watched Cord duck out the screen door. A crooked smile slowly curved Ronnie's lips.

Honey bent, her hand diving beneath the surf, her fingers closing over the colorful swirl of shell half buried in the sand. She loved these early-morning walks along the beach, collecting shells, breathing the sea air, watching the sun creep higher into the clear blue sky. It gave her peace, a kind of relaxed contentment with life and everything in it.

Straightening slowly, she examined the perfect little shell lying on her palm.

"Do you collect seashells?"

At Cord's question, Honey spun around in startled surprise, clutching the delicate shell in her palm. She wasn't used to having her early-morning walks interrupted. Seeing him standing a few feet away was even more disconcerting. He looked so disgustingly masculine with the breeze rippling his sable-dark hair and that arrogantly handsome face caressed and softened by the golden-orange rays of sunshine chasing across the shore.

"Yes, I collect shells, sometimes I even make things from them. Morning is the best time, you know." Honey's natural, husky drawl sounded breathy-soft and was almost whipped away by the wind and the surf.

Cord blinked in confusion. "Best time for what?" he rasped. The sight of her curvaceous form encased in tight, well worn cut-offs and a baggy pink T-shirt, damp from the sea spray and clinging to her breasts and abdomen, caused his body to react without hesitation. He had spent a better part of the night trying to deny what this woman could do to him. Now, all he could think of was the many things for which morning was the best time.

"The best time to collect shells," Honey replied, turning back to the shore and padding along the wet sand.

Cord remained where he was, watching the womanly sway of her hips, the way her legs looked. They were golden and firmly muscled, but tapered to feminine perfection. Her long braid struck her spine in rhythmic undulations, making him swallow convulsively. He couldn't help thinking that it should be illegal for someone that small to have that many curves in all the right places.

Cord shook his head, trying to rein in his wayward thoughts. He wasn't getting involved. Just last night, during the long hours when sleep wouldn't come, he'd arrived at that conclusion. He wasn't going to get involved! It was the way to avoid pain, the way to survive his time at the airshow. It was the only way.

"Honey . . ." Cord began briskly, his purposeful stride taking him to within three feet of her. Since she didn't stop to face him, he kept a little ahead of her. It was easier to talk without watching her body's movements.

"Yes," she murmured in response.

Cord's jaw clenched as his body reacted to the sound of her voice.

"What time will you be leaving for the hangar this morning?"

"About eight or eight-thirty. Our first show isn't until next month."

"Fine. I'll take that time to get an idea of just how you operate and what's going to be needed if I should decide to commit the funds for the airshow. From now on, we'll be staying near the hangar if you need us. That way we can drive out here only when necessary." If he could just keep it to business and avoid being alone with her, he knew he wouldn't have any complications he couldn't handle.

Puzzled at his abruptness, Honey found herself watching his movements. She couldn't help admiring his graceful saunter and the way his jeans pulled across the tautness of his backside. If ever a man had cute buns, it was he. Sighing, she shook her head. He had a cute everything, that was the problem.

"You can stay here. I've already told . . ." she began.

"No we can't," Cord snapped, stopping abruptly to face her.

Honey was given the choice of running into his chest, not a bad prospect, or stopping. She stopped.

"But . . ."

"Honey," Cord almost groaned. They were a mere foot apart, and every logical thought left his mind. Her breasts were obviously unencumbered by a bra, the nipples lovingly caressed by the damp T-shirt. He knew, without a doubt, she would have won that damn contest. He looked up and met her eyes. They were luminous, relaxed, and sexy. And her lips . . . They were full, moist, and slightly parted to continue her protests. It was more than a mortal man could take.

He had never professed to be anything but mortal.

All the reasons for staying away evaporated with the morning dew. The space between them disappeared, and once more, she was in his arms, pressed against his body. Only this time, comforting her was not his first priority. He knew he couldn't deny himself a taste of her lips any more than he could deny himself air.

His head lowered. Their lips met.

At the first brushing contact, Honey froze in startled surprise. But as his mouth settled over hers, as he gently brushed back and forth, seeking, sampling, she felt a tingling shock. Everything faded but Cord. Her trembling hands dropped the bag of shells she held. She never heard the clinking thud they made as they hit the sand. Instead, she heard the harshness of Cord's breath, and her hands moved to his shoulders. Honey stepped forward, her body instinctively cuddling closer to Cord's warmth.

Cord had thought one brief kiss would be enough, would satisfy his desire to know the feel of her lips. But one kiss *wasn't* enough. Her lips drew him back, again and again. Helplessly, he continued to brush her mouth with his own. His hands closed possessively on either side of her waist. When he felt her step forward, felt her lips part for him, he was lost.

He pulled her closer. His tongue brushed her lips before delving deeper to taste her. At the feel of her breasts against his chest, her hips snuggling closer, her tongue dueling with his own, a moan of emotion and need escaped his throat.

He wanted to lay her down on the soft, cool sand, to strip away the damp T-shirt, to see her breasts with their hard little peaks, peaks that were burning through two layers of fabric to sear his chest. He wanted to taste them, to know the saltiness of the ocean spray and the sweetness of Honey.

Cord's hand stroked toward the fullness of her breasts, spreading and bunching the damp cotton, until finally he cupped one breast. His other hand splayed across her lower back, just touching the curve of her bottom as he pulled her lower body closer and moved against her. It had been so long.

Honey moaned deep in her throat. It had been so long, too long since she felt like this. She was a woman again, wanted by a man. It felt good, his hand on her breast, his fingers moving over her nipple, his aroused body moving against her, his hair, his shoulders, his back, the deep, soul-stirring beauty of his kiss. It had been so long since she'd been loved like this, since she'd loved a man in return, but . . . this wasn't love.

Honey stiffened and pushed against Cord's hard chest. Her movements broke his sensual fog. He released her, staring at her as though he didn't know what had happened. The dazed passion in his hazel eyes slowly faded, and a shutter dropped, concealing his emotions from her.

Slowly, he turned away, but not before his eyes had noted every betraying tremor of her still-aroused body and the smoky darkness of her eyes.

"I . . . Honey, I'm sorry," he finally rasped.

"It wasn't all your fault," she offered. Her voice, too, was husky with the suppressed passions she felt. That she felt so strongly for this man surprised and appalled her. It wasn't like her.

"I apologize if my . . . behavior has caused a misconception . . ." he began. His first instinct had been the right one. He should have gotten away from here when he had the chance. She made him feel again, want again. She was nothing but trouble, and he had practically assaulted her on the beach!

"If you mean that this determines whether or not you help my show, then, no, I didn't misunderstand. I know I don't have to sleep with you to get your help. You wouldn't be as successful as you are if you did business that way."

Cord felt his muscles relax, and he felt a curious sense of pleasure. "Thank you, Honey. You're right," he continued as he turned back to face her. "This has no bearing on your show. I don't know why I . . . It won't happen again."

"I'm sorry, too. But it's okay. I . . ." Honey lowered her head and felt a heated blush spread over her cheeks. She sensed he was watching her, waiting for her to continue, to finish what she'd started to say. Oddly enough, she felt compelled to explain, to have him understand. His opinion of her mattered. It mattered a great deal.

"My husband died over two years ago. I haven't . . . I don't . . . There hasn't been anyone, and I guess I just got carried away."

Her revelation surprised him, but what surprised him more was the pleasure her admission gave him. He'd spent last night and this morning confused, trying to convince himself he wasn't going to get involved. Yet, knowing he was the first man to affect her this way since her husband's death gave him an almost primitive feeling of male satisfaction. It also made it easier for him.

"I—lost my fiancée over a year ago," Cord admitted softly.

Honey did look up this time. The catch in his voice,

and the way he said it, revealed a deeper meaning. She wasn't sure of that meaning until she saw his face. She understood. There hadn't been anyone for him, either.

"Then that's all it was, Cord," Honey concluded. It wasn't. She knew she was attracted to him, and had been since she saw him standing alone at the bar.

"Yes," he said, but a niggling doubt remained in the back of his mind. She could weaken his resolve just by standing next to him. How was he going to spend the next month in her company?

"And it won't happen again, at least not now that we understand it," she continued.

"Of course not."

"Besides, we have business to discuss."

"Yes, yes, of course we do."

"So, it won't happen again, right?"

"Right."

But when Honey bent to pick up her shells, and Cord saw her breasts sway with her movements, he swallowed with difficulty.

When Cord moved ahead of Honey down the beach, toward her beach house, she sighed.

"See you at the hangar," she called as she headed for the steps leading to her deck.

"Sure thing," Cord called back, giving her a casual wave.

Seeing the calloused palm of his hand sent a streak of stirring arousal through Honey's breasts. Quickly, she turned away and hurried up the stairs.

Cord's gaze was irresistibly drawn to Honey's hips and legs. He watched her climb the stairs and felt his body tense. Only after she disappeared inside did he turn away and head for the RV.

FOUR

When Honey arrived at the hangar, it was to find Cord's motor home set up to one side of the massive building. Both Cord and Ronnie were sitting in lawn chairs under a striped awning, and when they saw her get out of her aging dark-blue van, they stood and waited for her to reach them.

"Ready to meet the rest of the group?" Honey questioned as she stopped in front of them.

"Honey, I think I should warn you that there's usually a certain amount of hostility at the initial meeting . . ." Cord began.

"Cord, don't worry. My men understand the situation. I made sure of it. They've always stood by me."

"You may be right. But then again, they may resent my presence, or even think I'll get rid of them. I wanted you to be prepared."

Honey gave him an offhand, unworried thank-you, and Cord shrugged and fell into step behind her. He couldn't help noticing the way the sun turned her braided hair into liquid gold.

When they entered the hangar, both Cord and Ronnie

stayed in the background, giving Honey center stage. Carefully, Cord turned his attention to the other people in the hangar. Even if Honey was sure of his reception, he was reserving judgment.

"Okay, guys, let me have your attention for a minute."

Honey's raised voice carried through the echoing vastness of the hangar. Four men and two women stopped working and ambled toward her and the men standing behind her.

"This is Cord Wayne, and he'll be with us for a while . . ." Honey began, motioning to Cord as he stepped forward a pace.

"How long's a while?" Matt, her burly chief mechanic, asked.

Honey smiled fondly at the bear of a man in front of her, and he ducked his head in response. Cord almost laughed as one of the bear's giant paws pulled the baseball cap from his head, and the other reached up to scratch a bald spot surrounded by frizzled gray hair.

"He'll be here as long as it takes, until he decides if we're a good risk for his money."

"We're a dam- ah . . . dang good risk for his money," Billy Joe returned. The pilot gave Cord a belligerent glare, which Cord ignored.

"Well, we don't expect him to think so, just because we say so, do we?" Honey returned patiently. Billy Joe might be older than her by ten years, but he'd never managed to cool his temper. Her husband, Andy, once said that Billy Joe had saved his life, and for that, no matter what, he had a place with the show as long as he wanted it. So, Honey tried to exercise more patience with him than she would otherwise. Silently, she waited for his next move. But with one speculative look at her, and a final glare at Cord, he folded his arms over his chest, leaned one hip against a workbench, and waited.

"As I was saying, and please don't interrupt again, Cord will be here until he makes up his mind. That could be close to two months, well past our first show. I want you all to cooperate with him, answer his questions and the like. As I said before, this isn't a takeover, so don't get nervous. This will be a partnership, and any changes will be for the good of the show. Okay?"

Muttered grumbles were her only response. Stifling an exasperated sigh, she turned to Cord and gave a helpless shrug of her shoulders. He'd been right, but she really hadn't expected this reaction from her people.

"Okay, listen up!" Cord barked as he stepped up beside Honey.

The four men and two women in front of him perked up and shut up, mostly in shocked surprise.

"I have no intention of forcing you to do anything, but Ms. Johnson says she needs help to keep going. Are any of you questioning that?" Cord asked in a more normal tone of voice.

Heads shook in a negative response. No one questioned the authority in his voice.

"Okay then, we're all here to help out. I'll be looking over the operation, and I'll meet each of you and find out what you think could help the show. Then I'll see how the show's managed. If you're doing your jobs, you have nothing to fear from me; you're Ms. Johnson's family. But if you're hurting this show in any way and I decide to buy in, you're history. Do we understand each other?"

Cord could tell by the nods that he'd gotten through to them. Maybe now he'd be able to get answers instead of hostility. He always found that straight talking stopped the potential problems and rumors that usually ran through troubled businesses.

"Well, now, how about I introduce everyone?" Honey offered. Cord hadn't pulled his punches, and she respected that. But she was secretly amused by her people. They might argue with her, but not one of them said a word to Cord.

"First off, hiding back here is Ronnie Hunter. He's a friend of Cord's."

"And he also works with me," Cord offered.

Ronnie nodded once to the curious group but didn't attempt to leave his position in the background.

Honey smiled at Ronnie then continued her introductions. "Cord, this is Matt, my chief mechanic, Billy Joe and Rudy, the best aerobatic flyers in North Carolina, and Pete, my champion sky diver. Pete's also a pretty good pilot."

First Matt extended one hand, which engulfed Cord's. Billy Joe shook hands quickly, still showing a trace of anger. Next came Rudy, an older version of Pete, whose red hair showed a light dusting of gray at the temples. And then came Pete, the youngest of the group, who was a few years younger than Honey.

"It's nice to meet all of you. Rudy, are you Pete's father?" Cord asked, wanting to break the tension.

"Yep. I claim him on his good days, and his momma claims him on his bad ones," Rudy returned with an exaggerated drawl, giving Pete an affectionate cuff on the arm.

Everyone laughed before Cord turned to the two women standing with the men. He recognized one of them, and by her wide blue eyes, he assumed she remembered him as well. Honey shifted nervously at his side, and when he glanced down at her, he realized she hadn't told anyone about the incident in the tavern.

"And these ladies?" he asked casually.

"Evelyn and, umm . . . Sally," Honey said. "Evelyn's Billy Joe's wife. And Sally is Pete's fiancée. Right, Sally?" Honey hadn't gotten the chance to talk to Sally and only hoped she wouldn't blurt out the circumstances of her first meeting with Cord. She didn't want everyone to know what a fool she'd made of herself.

Sally looked from Cord to Honey, then back to Cord. "Soon as I can get him to pop the question," Sally finally said, directing a fond smile at the suddenly embarrassed Pete.

"Aw, Sal, why have I gotta ask you what you already know?"

" 'Cause I want roses and candy and you down on one knee," she promptly replied, directing a scolding frown at him when he faced her.

"You tell him, Sally," Pete's father, Rudy, said with a laugh.

Cord laughed, too, when he saw the chagrined, hangdog expression on young Pete's freckled face. Then, Cord paused. He'd forgotten how close people could get, and how good it felt to let them. Unconsciously, Cord took a step back, sobering as he watched the gentle ribbing Pete endured before he started teasing Billy Joe about his five kids.

"We been alone too long," Ronnie said from beside him, soft enough not to interrupt the others.

"What?" Cord turned to Ronnie in surprise, wondering what he was talking about with such authority.

"We don't fit in 'cause we ain't used to people anymore. This is how it was at your airfield, Tony razzin' you, you razzin' me. I wasn't used to it, either, at first, but you used to be." Ronnie shrugged and looked back at the small group now gathered around Honey.

Cord saw a hint of wistful longing in Ronnie's eyes, a desire to belong, and then it was gone. He sighed and reached up to rub the back of his neck with one hand. Why hadn't he ever realized how much Ronnie wanted to fit in? And why hadn't he remembered how it used to be?

Before Ronnie reminded him, he'd forgotten the teasing he'd endured at Wayne and Cray.

"Yes, I remember. There were good times . . ."

"Yeah. That's the trouble with trying to forget the bad ones, usually you forget the good ones, too."

"Cord, are you ready for a tour of the hangar and the airfield?" Honey called, breaking into their conversation. Her eyes were sparkling with laughter, a remnant of a joke one of the men had just told her. Her crew had moved away, returning to work, and she stood alone, waiting for Cord.

Cord was thoughtful as he turned away from Ronnie. "Sure, let's go," he responded. A few steps brought him to her side.

"We have one Cessna 152 Aerobat, mine," Honey began. "Rudy and Billy Joe both have Pitts Specials. Billy Joe's is a two-seater, and Rudy's is a home-built single-seater. Our jump plane is Matt's. It's a Cessna 180 six-seater. There's also my Staggerwing Beech, an antique my dad gave me when he had to quit flying. He has inner-ear problems," she answered before he could ask. "We use the Staggerwing for static displays and sometimes we do some simple rolls and loops with it . . ."

Honey talked as she walked, with Cord trailing behind her. In the hangar, he saw the antique gold-and-white biplane and the red jump plane with "Johnson's Jumpin' Fools" emblazoned in neon blue on each side. Outside, secured off the private runway, sat the white Cessna 152 Aerobat. It seemed almost plain compared to the two tricolored, custom painted Pitts Special biplanes parked on either side of it. All three were used for aerobatic demonstrations.

On the brief tour, Cord saw the well-organized work areas, the abundance of tools and materials, and the unused space and growth potential. He learned the format of the shows: aerobatic demonstrations, a certain amount of precision flying, and finally the skydivers, or "jumpers." On the ground, a static display of antique planes was set up for public viewing. It was a simple operation, and Cord was familiar with what was necessary to make it work. The tour didn't require all his concentration. He listened and asked questions, taking it in for future analysis, and another part of him began to stir with new life and remembered pleasure.

The smell of oil and fuel, the sound of metal on metal, the bantering shouts, the excitement in the air when a motor turned over, the sight of the planes gleaming in the bright sunlight, waiting for someone to make them soar, were all so familiar. And yet it was different. It had taken his absence from it for him to realize how much he loved it, how much he'd missed it. . . .

"And what we'd like to do is add a hang-gliding demo when we can. Jockey's Ridge State Park is known for hang gliding and would be a perfect spot."

"Jockey's Ridge?" Cord asked. The name caught his attention.

"It's the highest sand dune on the East Coast—about a hundred feet high. It's beautiful, with a view of the Sound, the beach, and the ocean. Actually, it's all sand, but as I said, the Ridge is perfect for hang gliding."

"And what other plans do you have?"

"Well, we want to add a glider or two, for demonstration and private instruction. For the shows, I'd like to get a wing walker—if we can find someone crazy enough to do it, and, finally, at least two hot-air balloons. But we need versatile people. My people all fly, three of us are experienced with aerobatic flying, most of us skydive, and at least two besides myself can work on the planes. Billy Joe has some experience with a balloon, but we haven't been able to afford one."

"Sounds ambitious, but not unrealistic," Cord said.

They reached her office, the last stop on the tour, and Cord was already starting to plan. He wasn't feeling the overwhelming depression he'd anticipated. He wasn't sickened by the hangar, the airfield, or the planes. Instead, he couldn't wait to delve deeper, to understand where Honey had gone wrong, or if she had gone wrong at all. It might be a while before he could go up in a plane, but at least he was thinking about it, even looking forward to it.

"Okay, so how . . ." he began as he opened the door marked "office." What he saw stopped him dead.

The light had been left on, thank heaven. Had he walked into the room in the dark, he might have fallen and broken his neck.

Cord grimaced as he looked around the room, and it failed to get any better. The small office was cluttered with papers and other paraphernalia. There were no windows, but an assortment of travel posters alleviated the wood-paneled walls.

In the center of the room, a squat brown thing practically sagged under the mound of papers, folders, magazines, and clippings piled on top of it. Though file cabinets were visible against the far wall, the one drawer he saw open was empty.

Cord stepped into the room, cautiously moving between two stacks of precariously balanced books. When he'd managed to take it all in, he turned back to find Honey braced in the doorway as though waiting for the axe to fall on her head.

Planting his fists on his hips, Cord cocked one brow in disapproval. "Are you sure this is your office? It looks like the local trash heap!"

"It's my office," she replied in a subdued voice. All the exuberance had gone out of her. The sparkling, exciting woman he'd been following all morning was gone.

Cord shook his head and glanced around again. The contrast between the rest of the hangar and this office was phenomenal. The contrast between her *house* and this office was even more phenomenal. No wonder she had invited him to her home instead of her office.

"How do you find anything?" Cord finally asked in patent disgust. As he moved out of the room, he accidentally brushed one of the stacks of books only to send it toppling over. When he escaped from her "office," he closed the door and leaned back against it, folding his arms over his chest.

Honey stood opposite him, far enough away to give him room, but close enough that he read the hopeless resignation in her eyes.

"I just manage to find it. I'm . . . I'm not good at this part of the business. Andy, my husband, was great at paperwork and organization." Honey sighed and met Cord's eyes across the space separating them.

She knew her office could be one of the main things wrong with the show. She knew she should have organized it long ago, but it never seemed that important. She always knew where everything was—well, for the most part—and she had hoped Cord would be willing to overlook it, maybe even laugh about it. But the disgust she saw disabused her of that notion. He was going to turn her down for sure. It was his first working day at the airfield; she should have waited.

Oh, well, no sense crying. "I'll understand if you plan to take off tonight. That office doesn't recommend me or my show. Maybe I should have waited, but . . ."

"It's better that you didn't. I'd have been angrier if you'd hidden it from me. Do you know what your bills are?" he questioned abruptly.

"Of course," she replied indignantly.

"And do they get paid? Do you know what you have in the bank?"

"Yes. And yes. They might not be on time, and they might not be paid in full, but I pay every month. The only thing I've actually lost is my International Council of Air Shows paperwork. But I know it's around here . . . somewhere."

Her honesty was a plus. She hadn't tried to hide anything from him. "Okay, we'll work on the rest. I'm going to spend two to three weeks just working with the men. You can start cleaning the office while I learn more about the show."

Cord turned away as he spoke and moved down the hall, toward the side door leading out of the hangar. Slowly, her surprise faded and she hurried after him before he left the building. She caught him at the door, just before he shut it behind him.

"You're not leaving?" she managed to pant breathlessly.

Cord stopped and looked over his shoulder, obviously surprised by her question. "Of course not. You asked me to evaluate the show. I'll evaluate it. And if I decide to buy in, you can damn well bet that office will be organized from A to Z."

"Thank you, Cord." Honey could barely speak past the sudden lump in her throat.

"Get the office clean," Cord returned with a fleeting smile. Then he was striding toward his RV. Halfway there, Ronnie joined him, seeming to appear out of nowhere.

Honey watched them for a moment before going back inside and closeting herself in her office. At that moment, she would have gladly gone down on her knees, if there had been any room on the floor.

Well, she had tried.

Honey sat in the chair behind what she fondly called

Mount St. Honey, and waited for it to start spewing books and papers over the rest of the office. Not that it would have made much difference. The rest of the office was almost as bad as her desk.

The worst part was, for the past three weeks, she'd faithfully spent four hours every day trying to clean the office. But it never seemed to look any better.

While Cord worked with each of her men for days at a time, she sorted trade magazines and articles. While Ronnie, who was a pretty good mechanic, worked exclusively with Matt, she shuffled papers and files. Each day brought their first airshow of the season that much closer, and each night brought out the office gremlins that seemed to increase the mess she was desperately trying to organize.

Her only respite came when she practiced for the show. It was then that she could lose herself in the vast blue sky she loved. It was also the only time she didn't feel guilty about her lack of progress. She knew Cord was going to come into the office one day, and she could imagine his reaction. No, actually, she didn't *want* to imagine his reaction. It was a miracle he hadn't been back to check on her.

Why wasn't she making any progress?

"Oh, what the heck!"

"You talkin' to yourself, half-pint?" Ronnie called from somewhere near the door.

Honey shook her head at the new nickname she had acquired, thanks to Ronnie, and stood up from behind her desk to see him over the clutter. She found Ronnie leaning against the doorjamb, observing the room, and her, with a devilish smile.

"I guess you could say that. I don't see why I'm not getting anywhere. Cord's going to think I'm incompetent. I can't even clean one room." She sighed, looking around in dismay.

"Is it really that important?"

Honey moved around the desk and headed toward the door. It was almost a relief that he'd interrupted. "Yes, it really is that important. It's the one thing Cord wanted me to do, and I can't seem to get it done."

Ronnie took another look around the room before turning back to Honey. "I could help. Looks to me like you need someone to get rid of the junk. Then you could get to the important stuff," he said as he shrugged his shoulders.

Honey didn't attempt to hide her surprise. Her eyes widened, and when she looked up to see if he was serious, she found his cheeks were tinged a dull red.

"Do you mean it?"

"Sure. Matt doesn't need me. And besides, you need the practice time. I just figured you could use some help."

"Thanks, Ronnie, I appreciate the offer, and I'll be happy to accept. To show my thanks for your services I'll take you up in one of the Cessnas whenever you want."

"No way!"

"What . . . ?" she began, confused by his vehement response.

"I ain't gettin' up in no plane."

"Why?"

"I just ain't," he declared militantly, glaring at Honey. His body was taut, no longer leaning against the doorjamb. His arms were held rigid at his sides, his fists clenched.

Honey chose not to take up the obvious challenge. Though she couldn't imagine anyone refusing a plane ride, she had no desire to lose the one offer of help she'd had. Why he was offering, she had no idea, but she thought it was a sweet gesture.

"Okay, Ronnie, I withdraw the offer. Are you still willing to help out in here?"

"Sure. I said I was. You go on and do what you gotta do," he replied, instantly relaxing now that she'd dropped the subject of flying.

"Well, okay, but I still want to offer you something. How about a real home-cooked meal?"

"You bet!" Ronnie exclaimed, a lopsided smile lighting his face.

"Tonight?"

"Excellent. Uh, Cord's been shopping again, and I saw the freezer's full."

Honey chuckled, knowing that particular sight was not a welcome one. Ronnie had the deepest appreciation for any meal that didn't come in a divided plate.

"Okay, six-thirty, my house, and I'll find Cord and talk to him."

"Allll right," Ronnie drawled happily. "And don't worry about this place, I'll have it overhauled in no time."

"Okay, I won't. Thanks again, Ronnie." As Honey moved around him to leave the office, Ronnie's hand on her arm stopped her.

She looked up in question and found his brows drawn together in a serious frown. His deep-blue eyes were oddly grave and concerned.

"You don't need to worry. I know Cord wouldn't hold this mess against you. You run a pretty good show, and everything else is in real prime condition. He's seen that."

Honey smiled tenderly, and on impulse, she stood on tiptoe and pulled his head a little closer to plant a brief kiss of thanks on his cheek. When she moved into the hall, she turned back and saw the rather dazed wonder on his young-old face before he disappeared into the office.

In the past three weeks, she had found Ronnie to be an unusual young man. He was cocky and tough on the outside, but he could also be considerate and kind. She didn't believe he was the twenty-one he claimed. He seemed younger, at least until his eyes clouded as though he'd seen too much of life's dark side. When he wasn't working with Matt, Ronnie often sought her out to lend a hand, and she had come to enjoy his company, and his teasing. Cord, however, didn't seek her out. In fact, they hadn't been alone together since his first day at the hangar, which had been fine with her. She hadn't wanted to face any questions about her office.

Honey found Cord outside, inspecting her Cessna. He seemed almost reverent as he touched one of the wings.

"Hello, Cord," she called as she approached.

Cord spun around at the sound of her voice, looking startled, then guilty, as if he'd been doing something he shouldn't.

"I'm sorry, I didn't mean to startle you," she said with a smile, stopping a few feet away from him.

"It's okay. I was thinking of something else and didn't hear you. How's the office coming?" He turned back toward the plane, but he made no move to continue whatever he had been doing.

"Ronnie's offered to help, and . . ."

"Ronnie? Ronnie's offered to *clean*?" he questioned in disbelief. He turned to look at her, and quickly forgot why he'd done so. Helplessly, his gaze wandered over her face, watching the smile come to her eyes and then curve her lips before she laughed. The sound of her laughter sent ripples of sensation through his body. Cord's jaw clenched.

"Actually," Honey began, "I felt the same way when he offered to clear out the junk. But he'll leave the important stuff for me to go through. I think it'll work out fine."

"No doubt," Cord replied absently, having only a vague idea of what their conversation was about. "He's a good kid, kind of rough around the edges if you're not used to him, but a good kid nonetheless."

"I know. Oh, uh, I offered to cook dinner for Ronnie, to thank him. You're invited, too."

Cord didn't say anything for a full two seconds. With a rather unfathomable look, he turned away. "Thanks for the offer," he finally said, still without facing her.

"Your first show is next week, and your people seem ready." Cord changed the subject, managing not to answer her invitation. He didn't want to talk about dinner. He would be content to continue on as they had these past three weeks, with as little personal contact as possible. Her offer of dinner was unexpected, and even though he knew Ronnie would be there, it didn't help. The beach house, the ocean, the moonlight, and Honey, a combination created to drive a man crazy, to drive *him* crazy.

Up to now, he had managed to avoid being alone with her. He knew the desire to continue in that vein was stupid and unrealistic. He knew he'd have to deal closely with her eventually, but he didn't want eventually to be today. He wasn't ready.

It hadn't taken long for him to realize how he had fooled himself. Thoughts of that morning on the beach, when he'd kissed and held her, still tormented him. Whenever he looked at her, he felt his body stirring in response. Even now, out here in the open, he wanted to take her in his arms again. He was obsessed with her. He couldn't be in the same room without wondering if her lips would taste the same, or her body would . . .

"I've got a good bunch of people working for me. We'll continue practicing until then, and by show time, everything will run like clockwork. My crew's always put on an excellent show," Honey replied proudly, pulling Cord's thoughts back to the airshow.

"So, tell me what you think so far?" she continued, looking at him expectantly.

Cord was happy to have something else to concentrate on.

"I've spent a lot of time with the men, and they know what they're doing. Matt, Rudy, and Pete have been nothing but cooperative. Billy Joe, on the other hand, has an attitude problem. Where'd that chip on his shoulder come from?"

"I don't know. But I think you'll find he mellows on acquaintance. He's got a pretty large family, and he works hard at two different jobs, three when we're off-season. He's probably just afraid you're going to get rid of him."

"Well, for now, don't worry. I'll be working with him this afternoon and a little bit tomorrow. We'll just have to see."

"Okay," Honey replied, a trace of worry in her voice. With a shake of her head, she put Billy Joe out of her mind. She knew, eventually, Billy Joe would accept Cord as the others had.

"Cord, do you think you could give me an idea when you'll make your decision?" she asked, directing a winsome, pleading look at him.

Cord reluctantly smiled in response. His gaze met her own, and laugh lines appeared at the corners of his hazel eyes. "Are you pushing me?"

"Me?" Honey returned in wide-eyed disbelief. "I'd never think of pushing a big businessman like you."

"Uh-huh." Cord nodded, then chuckled when she shifted her weight from one foot to the other and tried to look nonchalant.

"Well, maybe if you gave me a hint?" she wheedled, giving him her best smile.

Cord's breath caught at the smile she flashed him. The teasing mischief, warmth, and beauty of that smile would have frozen any man and then melted him into an acquiescent puddle.

"How about I give you my answer after your first show?" he offered.

"Really?" Honey's eyes sparkled in pleasure.

"Yes, really. However, we've got to find your books so I can take a look at them."

"No problem," Honey replied confidently. She wanted to hug him, but she knew that wasn't a good idea, not after she'd practically melted when she heard his deep, sexy chuckle.

Cord turned back to the Cessna as though pulled by an invisible rope. Obviously, their conversation was supposed to be over, but Honey couldn't make herself leave. He hadn't gone up in a plane in the past three weeks. She knew he'd been busy, but he seemed to avoid going up in the air. Like with Ronnie, she found she wanted to do something special for Cord.

"How about I take you up in my Cessna tomorrow?" she offered.

This time, she didn't startle him, but he looked surprised at the suggestion. She didn't know if it was her continued presence that surprised him or the question.

I can't, he said, but only to himself. Over a year had passed since Gina's death, and since he'd last flown. Would he discover he now hated flying as much as Ronnie did?

"Sure. How about two in the afternoon? I'm going over the repair records with Matt tomorrow morning," Cord said in reply.

"Two P.M. it is then," Honey agreed. She turned to walk back to the hangar with an undeniable sense of triumph.

Cord watched Honey until she disappeared into the building. He looked up into the clear blue sky. The day seemed to have gotten darker somehow. With a sigh, he lifted one hand to rub the back of his neck. He turned, shoved his hands into his back pockets, and began walking down the runway. One thing was certain. He had no intention of going to Honey's beach house for dinner.

FIVE

How had he gotten talked into this? It wasn't as if he didn't have food in the freezer. It wasn't as if he'd asked to join Ronnie. It wasn't as if he really wanted to go.

He'd refused the first time Ronnie asked him, and the second, and the third. Ronnie hadn't given up, or given in, easily. Next thing he knew, he was helping Ronnie secure the RV for the drive to Honey's. He still wasn't sure why. He told himself it was because they needed to talk about the show, and he even started to believe it.

Dusk was approaching, the breeze off the ocean had a chill to it, and Honey was frying chicken and humming in the kitchen. He could hear her from the deck, where he sat in one of the natural wood loungers with its off-white, gray-striped cushion. He could only imagine the smell of the chicken by the crackle of grease he heard each time the swinging kitchen door swished back and forth.

Cord had gladly banished himself from the house shortly after arriving. One look at Honey in her snug, hip-hugging jeans and the royal-blue oversize sweater that kept sliding off her shoulder had been enough for him. It was all he could do to stay away from her when she looked so damn cuddly. But staying on the deck, in the cool early-evening breeze, was doing nothing to help his crumbling control. All his reasons for staying away from her seemed unimportant next to the clamoring demands of his body.

He could close his eyes and see the smooth golden skin of her shoulder, her very bare shoulder. She wasn't wearing a bra. The sweater had been large enough that that fact wasn't obvious, and maybe it didn't matter to half of the population—the female half. But he knew what lay under her sweater. He'd seen her in a wet T-shirt, twice. He'd touched her. He ached to touch her again. It was all he could do not to boot Ronnie out the front door and strip that sweater off Honey. His fist clenched, and his arm tensed against the wood of the lounger. Just the thought of having Honey, alone, without her sweater, was enough to heat his blood.

Her hair had been loose when he came in, and she'd been in the process of tying it back. It was as he'd imagined it would be, a glorious mane of gold, just waiting for a man's hands—his hands. He'd wanted to tell her to leave it loose. He had wanted to run his fingers through her hair, from her scalp to her hips, to caress her body at the same time.

Cord closed his eyes and groaned deep in his throat. He had to stop thinking like this. He had to combat the attraction he felt for her, an attraction that seemed to grow each time she came near him. No matter how many times he told himself it was too soon to get involved, that he didn't want to risk getting hurt again, his body seemed to feel otherwise. Three weeks had done nothing to cool his response. Just the opposite.

He'd seen her daily, had watched her with her employees, listened to her giving instructions in her clear, direct way. He'd seen her smooth over ruffled feathers, and leave both parties smiling as she walked away. He'd heard her laughing at a joke, or at Pete's antics, from across the hangar, and her laughter had made him smile. Each day, he'd looked forward to seeing her, almost as much as he dreaded it. And each time he saw her, he wanted her more. She didn't try to be sexy. She didn't try to attract him. She didn't have to. Her appeal was natural, an innate part of her, and all the more dangerous for just that reason. She played havoc with his hard-won control, and she didn't even realize it.

Raising his glass of ginger ale, which Honey had thoughtfully brought him after he'd gone out onto the deck, Cord slid the cool, wet surface over his forehead. Honey was slowly driving him crazy. He took a sip of the refreshing drink, then looked down at the glass. In his mind, he saw that special sweet smile he would always associate with Honey. She'd smiled at him when she handed him the glass. Lord, was he in trouble. How the hell was he going to get out of this house, this state, with his sanity intact? Cord set his glass down on the deck, leaned back, and closed his eyes.

Honey smiled as she carefully slid the screen open and stepped out onto the deck. Cord looked like he was sleeping. The sound of the surf masked her footsteps as she moved closer. She sank down onto the wooden frame of the lounger and reached out to touch Cord's shoulder.

"Cord?" she called softly. He opened his eyes and looked deeply into her own. The intense, compelling fire in his eyes caused her to catch her breath. Instinctively, she pulled her hand back.

"I'm sorry. I just wanted to let you know dinner is almost ready. I've got Ronnie watching the timer for the rolls."

"No problem. I was just resting and enjoying the

ocean,'' he replied, closing his eyes to escape the glowing warmth her presence created.

A strong breeze lifted her hair, where it lay on her shoulder, and blew it toward Cord's face before she could grab hold of it.

"Sorry." Honey tried to subdue her blowing hair, but seeing the frown cross his brow, she grew concerned. What could be bothering him if not worries over her show? Several strands of hair broke free of her hold and lightly floated around them.

Cord fought the urge to reach for her. He wanted her hair to surround him. He wanted to bury his hands in the silky flower-scented mass, to pull her close, to . . . He heard the unconscious groan that came from deep within him. Quickly, he cleared his throat, trying to mask that telling sound.

"What's wrong, Cord? Are you feeling okay? Is anything wrong?"

"I'm fine. I'm just working things out in my head," he replied, his voice husky and strained. He felt her hair skim across his cheek, felt it catch in the rough stubble of his evening beard. He didn't open his eyes. He knew what she'd see if he did. He didn't move because he couldn't. It was sweet torment to have her close to him, a torment he was finding addictive. What he'd avoided for three weeks was also what he'd craved—Honey, alone, with him.

"Can I help?" she questioned softly as she instinctively leaned closer.

Cord opened his eyes and looked directly into hers. Fiery hazel met concerned brown. There was something in his look, something untamed. Honey blushed. Her hair slipped out of her hand, and when she tried to catch hold of it, Cord stopped her. The burning touch of his hand on hers stilled her.

More strands of her hair moved around them, seemingly with a life of their own. Cord reached behind her, his eyes never leaving hers. He unfastened the metal clip at the base of her neck, and Honey felt her hair lift, fluffing out because of the swirling air currents on the deck. She heard the clip hit the wooden deck and didn't care. The pleasure in Cord's eyes made her breath catch.

She watched him lean forward, watched him lift his other hand. She felt his hands in her hair, on both sides of her head. Her eyes closed. In slow motion, he buried his fingers in her hair. Her lips parted on a silent breath. Heat coursed through her, as devastating to her control as a hurricane to the unprotected coastline.

Honey felt the gentle pressure of his hands pulling her closer. She moved into his arms without a thought of protest. She felt his lips on hers, tentative, gentle. Her breath quickened in anticipation, her hands went to his shoulders, then around his neck as he leaned back, taking her with him. The kiss deepened.

It felt so right to be in his arms again. No matter how much she had tried to convince herself that their first kiss was a mistake, she knew she'd been lying. She still wanted him. Each day at the hangar, she watched for a glimpse of him, and the sound of his voice was enough to make her feel warm and melting inside. There was no explanation, no logical reason, nothing to tell her what she felt was right. But she knew what she felt in Cord's arms was real, something that defied description. When his tongue traced her bottom lip, she allowed him access.

Honey moaned as his tongue met and mated with her own. Her breasts swelled against his chest. She felt the tightening in her abdomen, the aching heat that gathered there. Why did this one man have such power over her? She wanted to lose herself in his arms, wanted to forget the airshow, the world. When his hand slid down to cup her breast, she did.

Cord couldn't get enough of her sweet mouth. He kissed her as if he were starving for the taste of her, as if he'd been hungry since that one brief kiss so many weeks ago. But the taste of Honey was addictive. He wanted more.

His hand moved down, away from the silky-sweet bondage of her hair twining around his fingers. He felt the smooth warmth of her neck, her collarbone. He felt the kittenish tickle of her sweater, and then his hand cupped the fullness of her breast. He heard her moan, felt the hardened peak against his palm, and fire surged into his loins.

He wasn't thinking, he didn't care about today, tomorrow, or yesterday. His one thought, his only thought, was of the responsive woman in his arms. His lips left hers, trailing down her neck, under her chin. He felt her shudder in his arms.

He wanted all of her. He wanted to see, touch, taste, every inch of her. With no thought of where they were, his fingers caught in the top of her sweater, pulling it off her shoulder. He lowered it further, until her breast was bare to his appreciative gaze. His eyes roamed over her perfection, the creamy skin and hard pink crest. With another groan, this one of pleasure, he took her nipple into his mouth. Honey whimpered, and he felt her fingers pull at his hair, felt her nails dig into his scalp.

"Come and get it before I eat it all!" Ronnie yelled from inside the beach house.

Cord jerked back to reality as if doused with ice water. He wanted to punch something, preferably Ronnie. Seeing the fiery passion in Honey's dark eyes recede as confusion took over brought Cord to his senses. He tugged her sweater back into place with a gentle motion he didn't even think she felt. With the same care, he pushed her into a sitting position and brought her hands down to rest on her lap. She swayed, and he steadied her. Seeing her well-kissed mouth and the light blush on her cheeks made him want to kiss her again, to go on kissing her, caressing her, until neither of them could think, until all his reasons for staying away from her seemed insignificant. With a jolt of surprise, Cord realized that had already happened.

He hadn't thought of where they were, who could see them, who she was, why he should stay away. He had thought of nothing once Honey was in his arms. He was a fool.

She looked so lost. Seeing her struggle for control snapped Cord out of his own self-recriminations. What was she thinking?

"Are you okay, Honey?" Cord asked. His voice was so strained, he wasn't sure she could hear him.

Honey felt as though she'd been snatched away from heaven. She took a deep breath and tried to get her pulse to stop racing. Her body throbbed. She could feel an ache deep inside, and when she focused on Cord, when she looked into his concerned eyes, she felt shame. How could she have allowed things to go so far? Why hadn't she stopped him?

"I'm . . . I'm fine. I don't know . . . I—" Honey broke off, unable to meet his eyes, unsure of what to say. What must he think of her?

"In his own unique way, Ronnie said dinner was ready. We'd better go in before he makes good on his threat. You'd be amazed at how much food he can put away." Cord slid off the opposite side of the lounger and stood. He ran his fingers through his wavy dark-brown hair to try to tame it. Then, he came around, opened the sliding screen, and looked back at her.

Honey stood and moved toward the door automatically. A frown wrinkled her brow as she tried to come to terms with the torrid kiss they'd shared. Cord was acting as though it had never happened. In fact, if it weren't for the bruised feel of her lips and her hypersensitive breasts, she could almost believe she had just had a very detailed fantasy.

When she reached the open screen, she could see Ronnie, already seated at the dining-room table, his plate almost overflowing with food. Honey stopped and looked up at Cord. She saw the sheen of sweat beading his upper lip and brow. She saw the banked flames in his eyes, the way his breathing increased with her nearness. At least she was not the only one affected.

"Cord, what just happened . . . What are we going to do?" she asked softly, so Ronnie wouldn't hear.

"We aren't going to *do* anything, Honey," he replied in his deep velvety voice.

"But why did it . . ."

"Our first kiss wasn't a fluke, or just circumstance. You know that as well as I do. What we have, well, it's some pretty powerful chemistry. What just happened proves that. But we also have a business relationship which has to take precedence. I want to assure you that what happened out here won't happen again."

And it damn well wouldn't if he had anything to say about it. How could he have forgotten the reasons he didn't want to get involved with another woman, any woman, and especially one like Honey? Perhaps he really was going crazy. He had no other explanation.

"It won't?" she asked hesitantly, lowering her eyes once before she met his gaze again. She tried to mask her thoughts, to hide them from Cord. He was so adamant about keeping things "strictly business" between them. But the thought of never kissing him again was oddly distressing.

"No, Honey. I have a job to do, we both do, if you

expect help with your show. I can't make you guarantees on the show, but I can assure you that you are safe from me.'' Was he trying to convince her, or himself. He didn't know anymore.

"I understand, Cord, but I have never felt 'unsafe' with you. I want you to know something.''

"What?''

"I wouldn't just . . . I mean I don't just . . .'' How did she say she wasn't the kind of woman who indulged in this type of thing when she'd already shown she *was*, not once, but twice with him. And if he were willing, she had no doubt she'd fall into his arms again.

"Believe it or not, I understand. What happens between us is . . . Shall we eat now?'' he asked in an obvious attempt to change the subject.

"Yes, of course. You must be hungry.'' Honey could have bitten her tongue off. She could feel herself blushing, but thankfully, Cord didn't comment.

She turned and entered ahead of him. When she met Ronnie's rather questioning look, she wanted to drop through the floor. She had forgotten what she must look like. Her hair was all tangled around her, her mouth probably showed the evidence of her passionate encounter with Cord, and she was just starting to feel the sensitive area on her neck where Cord's hair-roughened cheek and jaw had nuzzled her.

Ronnie didn't say a word. He turned back to his plate, and Honey saw the shaking of his shoulders. She reached him first and took the seat across from him. One look at his face and she realized he was trying very hard not to laugh himself silly. Honey kicked him under the table.

"Dammit!'' Ronnie exclaimed, his surprised eyes coming up to meet Honey's sweet, innocent expression.

"Ronnie . . .'' Cord began as he took his seat.

"Hey, it wasn't my fault. Talk to half-pint," Ronnie shot back.

Cord turned to look at Honey, who met his look with an expression that clearly said, "Who, me?", and Cord chuckled. He didn't say another word, just started filling his plate. The chicken, mashed potatoes and gravy, rolls, and mixed vegetables, looked and smelled delicious. Though he would be the last one to admit it, after his defense of frozen dinners, he loved home-cooked meals as much as Ronnie did.

Both Honey and Cord began eating, and it wasn't until their mouths were full that Ronnie decided it was safe to talk.

"This stuff tastes a lot better than that cardboard stuff you're always fixin'," he drawled.

Cord glared at him, and Ronnie just smiled.

"Yep, I figure we ought to stick around here just for the food. 'Course, maybe there's another reason and . . . Ouch!" Ronnie cried. He bent over to rub his shin and glared at Cord.

"Maybe if you keep eating this food you're raving about, you'll find it easier to walk away from the table," Cord commented.

"Yeah, right."

Honey hid her amusement, knowing Ronnie might not appreciate it. "Cord, how did you get started investing in small businesses?" she asked politely.

"It just happened. We started traveling, and when we stopped in a small town in Virginia, I found a restaurant that had the best Italian food I've ever tasted. They were ready to shut down because they couldn't get customers. I offered to evaluate their business and helped them find ways to reduce their costs and increase their advertising. They needed some money, and after talking to my partner and my dad, we decided to try investing in the business and see what happened. That particular restaurant was just written up in a national magazine for its excellent cuisine. I've been lucky. I can usually spot a good investment. I've found I'm good at evaluating the strengths and weaknesses of a small business.''

"You mentioned your partner and your dad?" Honey took another bite of chicken, her eyes never leaving Cord.

"Yes," Cord continued after he swallowed another bite of food. "I started working part-time for Antony Cray when I was sixteen. It was one of the best moves I ever made; he taught me a lot. My dad, Leland, owned a helicopter-tour business, and I flew some tours once I got my license. After Dad sold the business, I went to work full-time for Antony. As I grew older, and started designing planes, Antony and I became partners. Then, when I decided to travel, my dad took over my job. It gave him something to do with his spare time."

It felt good to talk about Antony and his father. Cord had avoided it for the past year, thinking the memories would bring him pain, but they didn't. It was yet another pleasant surprise to realize that fact.

"And your mom?" Honey questioned, having heard nothing of the woman who raised him.

"Mom died when I was fourteen. She had a heart attack and just passed away one afternoon while she was napping."

His unemotional tone didn't fool Honey. She saw the residual pain in the depths of his hazel eyes. She reached over and covered Cord's hand with her own. "I'm sorry."

Cord's gaze focused on her, and his hand turned over to clasp hers and give it a squeeze.

"Thank you," he said, his husky voice low and intimate. His gentle smile warmed her.

"You got a television?" Ronnie broke in to ask.

Honey pulled her hand from Cord's and looked across

the table. She was embarrassed to realize she'd been rude to Ronnie. She'd been practically ignoring him.

"No, I'm sorry. I'm not usually home long enough to watch TV."

"No problem."

"I wanted to thank you again for your help in my office, Ronnie," she offered.

"Yeah, well, you needed someone to help you out," Ronnie returned, but he didn't look up. He kept fidgeting with his fork.

"There's pie in the refrigerator."

That got his attention. Ronnie looked up and met her eyes.

"Homemade?"

"Well, not by me. Rudy's wife baked it and sent it home with me. It's apple, and there's ice cream in the freezer."

"Allll right!"

Without another word, Ronnie left the table and disappeared into the kitchen.

"You're learning how to deal with him. Offer him food and he's happy," Cord said with a chuckle. He folded his napkin and placed it on the table by his plate.

"I felt bad for ignoring him. He seemed so . . . I don't know, *uncomfortable*." Honey, too, had finished eating. She placed her napkin on the table and sat back, not yet ready to start clearing.

"Probably the subject matter. Ronnie isn't one to include himself in a conversation. He listens. I'm sure sometimes he gets homesick. The airfield is where he grew up, and Antony is like a father to him." Cord offered, his voice gentle and reassuring.

"I just hope he's not upset with me. I wouldn't hurt him for the world."

"Half-pint, you wouldn't hurt anyone 'for the world.'

You didn't hurt my feelings. I was done eatin', that's all. I'm not used to your house. It's . . . uh . . . silent.''

Honey looked around and realized it was more than that. Her eyes widened in shock as she tried to see her home the way they saw it. It looked like a hotel room. Even the most simple memorabilia, like a picture of her family, was absent. No wonder Ronnie was uncomfortable here. He was a young man, probably used to television and rock music. She used to have a television. She used to collect things, before Andy died and she'd moved out of their house and into this one. But that had been two years ago. Why had she never realized how . . . barren this place was? It wasn't really a home at all.

''I'm sorry. I . . .'' Honey began, embarrassed by her realizations.

''Can I help you clear?'' Cord asked quietly, standing as Ronnie sat down with his plate of pie and ice cream.

Honey looked up and found Cord watching her; she lowered her head. Following his lead, she stood and started clearing the table.

Cord followed Honey into the kitchen and stacked his dirty dishes on the counter. He watched Honey move around the room, putting food in smaller containers, covering them, and placing them in the refrigerator.

''It was a good meal. Thank you for inviting me.''

''You're welcome.'' She replied automatically, moving to stand by the sink.

''Are you okay?''

''Sure.''

''No, you're not.'' Cord stepped up behind her and placed his hands on her shoulders, turning her to face him.

''Cord, I need to run the dishwater.'' Honey moved to try to break his hold.

''Leave it. I want to know what's wrong. Ronnie said

it was silent here, and you changed. Now tell me what's wrong.''

"Nothing."

"Well, I'm a patient man; I'm willing to wait here most of the night. It's not like I have to drive home. I happen to drive my home around with me," Cord replied reasonably.

Honey tried not to smile but couldn't help it. Cord, in this mood, was irresistible. Her smile peeked through.

"That's better. Now, tell me what happened."

"I just realized how ill-equipped my house is to deal with company, and, well, it embarrassed me a little." She ducked her head and refused to look up at him as she made the admission.

"Don't be embarrassed. Ronnie tends to get restless unless there's some noise to distract him. I think your house is very peaceful." *Like a nuclear meltdown is peaceful*, but Cord couldn't say that. It wasn't her fault he reacted whenever they were within ten feet of each other, or for that matter within the same room. He didn't want her hurt. He didn't want to see the light go out of her velvety-brown eyes. He wanted to protect her, to make her sparkle with light and laughter again. That thought alone sobered him.

"Thank you, Cord." His concern was unexpected, and it gave her a warm, cared-for feeling.

"Do you want some help cleaning up in here?"

"No. Why don't you keep Ronnie company, and I'll get the rest of the dishes. I can serve dessert now if you wish."

"No. Unlike Ronnie, I can wait a bit."

Cord released her and moved away. He knew he should refuse dessert and just leave, but he didn't want to. Once more, he tried to tell himself it was because they needed to talk about the show.

"Honey, when you're finished in here, we need to discuss the show."

Honey looked up, wary because of the sudden brisk tone of his voice. His impassive expression did nothing to reassure her. "Sure, Cord. I'll be done in just a few minutes. Would you like some coffee?"

"Yes, thank you. When you have time."

His extreme politeness was yet another disturbing note. Honey tried to tell herself she was imagining more than was there. As she ran soapy water into the sink, she even half convinced herself she was right.

Cord left the kitchen and bypassed the table, and Ronnie, to go into the living room. He stood looking out the window, at the moonlight reflecting off the ocean. With a sigh, he raised his hand to rub the base of his neck.

"Problems?" Ronnie asked from beside him. Cord hadn't even heard him approach.

"Yes."

"With the show, or with Honey?"

Cord slowly turned to look at Ronnie. Ronnie met his look, his blue eyes serious, his young-old face worried.

"Both I'm afraid."

SIX

"Where's Ronnie?" Honey asked as she entered the living room carrying the coffee service and cups on a large silver tray. She placed the tray on the coffee table.

"He went out to the RV. He said to tell you he'd see you later. He was tired and wanted to lie down," Cord said in reply. He turned and walked over to take one of the plush blue-gray chairs and help himself to a cup of coffee.

"I think he was not so much tired as in need of a little diversion—like a television." After pouring herself a cup of coffee, Honey curled one leg under her and sank onto one of the flowered sofa cushions. She looked over at Cord, and caught a hint of a smile curving his lips. Then, his brief smile became a memory, and she felt the loss.

"So, what do we need to talk about?"

Cord sat back in the chair and met her questioning gaze across the rattan coffee table. He paused a moment to sip his hot coffee before he replied.

"I want to tell you what conclusions I've come to so far. There are some very real problems," he finally said.

Honey sat forward, a worried frown creasing her brow.

Warily, she watched Cord. He seemed so remote, so unap-
proachable. It chilled her, especially after what they had
shared before dinner. But she couldn't think of that now.
She had to think of her air show.

"Okay, tell me what the problems are?"

"First, I want to ask you something. Why don't you
just sell the airshow, Honey? Why keep it when what you
really prefer, what you really love, is the flying?" Cord's
voice was gentle, his eyes clear and direct, ripping to the
heart of the matter faster than anyone else had ever dared.

She didn't know what to say. Hadn't she often wondered why she kept holding on, and struggling, just to
make ends meet? Didn't she sometimes hate dealing with
the problems, trying to keep the peace, trying to keep
equipment running for just a little while longer?

And then, each day she walked in and saw the dear
faces of the people who depended on her, who probably
couldn't find a job elsewhere, at least not doing the thing
they loved most. She knew how they felt, knew she could
never survive cooped up in a building all day, away from
the air and sunshine. The airshow was a dream, a dream
that she and her husband had tried to make come true.

Since Andy's death, it had seemed more like a night-
mare at times, but those times passed. Why didn't she
sell? She could no more sell the show and walk away than
she could command her heart to stop beating or her mind
to stop the endless yearning to soar thousands of feet off
the ground. Would he understand, could he?

"I can't sell, Cord. The airshow is a part of me. People
depend on me—good people."

"People who could work elsewhere, like you. Wouldn't
you be happier without the worry?" He was stating facts
and asking questions without the slightest hint as to his
own feelings. He neither demanded she agree or disagree.

"Yes . . . No . . . Maybe. I don't know. Sometimes I

feel overwhelmed, but those times pass. I can't imagine what I would do without the airshow. It was Andy's dream . . ."

"But is it *your* dream?" Cord cut her off, making her take a step back before she answered, making her think of things she'd never put into words before. It had started out as Andy's dream, and she had continued to think of it that way, even after he died. But now . . .

"Yes. It's my dream now," she said with conviction. "I love the show, and the people who work for me are family." And she realized all she said was true.

Honey took a sip of her coffee and watched Cord nod acceptance of her answer. Had he needed to hear her say it? Or had he known she needed to say it, to understand it was true? She had never realized that the dream had become hers in the past two years, not until she said the words. How had Cord known that?

"The management side of your business is lacking," Cord said bluntly, breaking into her thoughts.

"I told you, Andy was always . . ."

"Andy isn't here anymore. You need to hire a manager, or you have to let your husband go and take on the management job yourself," Cord stated.

Honey winced and grew silent. She stared at Cord and waited for what would come next. She watched him, her eyes round and revealing a trace of hurt feelings. Her body tensed as if to accept a blow.

Cord sighed and set his cup back on the coffee table. He stood and began to pace from the fireplace to the sliding-glass doors and back again.

"What else?" Honey asked, surprised at how brittle her voice sounded in the silent room.

Cord stopped and gripped the back of his chair. His intense hazel eyes pinned her in place. "If you can't handle the evaluation, you shouldn't have asked me to stay, to look at your show.''

''I never said I couldn't handle it. But my show has a lot of potential, I know it does.''

''Yes, and I've seen it. But I can be objective, more so than you, and I can see the problems with your show, problems I don't think you've been willing to face.''

''I face problems, Cord. I know what's wrong with the show. We need money. That's why I called your office,'' she explained with forced patience.

''You need a hell of a lot more than money. You need good management and public relations. You need at least one office clerk or someone competent enough to run your business. You need diversity and a more comprehensive show. You need to look fancy and be the best to convince the public that they'd be lucky if you agreed to do a show for them,'' Cord shot back.

''I . . .''

''I know you've realized some of these things, but there are many things besides money that make a business successful.''

''I know that.'' Honey set her coffee cup on the table and leaned forward, meeting Cord's eyes. ''If there's something I don't know, I can learn. I'm trying to get my office organized, and money is a big part of why I can't hire more people, can't diversify, can't look fancy.''

''If you don't have the proper people in place, and the right attitude, all the money in the world won't save your show. You won't survive unless you're able to take on the management responsibilities or get someone else who can.''

''I can do it,'' Honey said doggedly.

''Can you fire someone, one of your 'family'?''

''There's no need. My people are good . . .'' she defended, her voice heating with anger

"You have one person who lets their personal problems and hang-ups upset the hangar and everyone else working there," Cord stated.

Honey's growing anger was momentarily halted. She looked at him in question. "Who?"

"Billy Joe."

Honey shook her head in denial. "No. I know he's a bit stubborn, but he's good at—"

"Good at having an attitude problem."

"Cord . . ." she began, trying to stay calm. "Billy Joe has a lot of problems, that's true. The biggest is the fact he's slow to accept change. He . . ."

"He'll have to go if I agree to invest in your show," Cord stated without emotion, never moving from his spot behind the chair.

Honey's stricken eyes met his cool, unwavering gaze. This was not the man she had thought she was getting to know. This man was rock-hard, uncompromising.

"No," she whispered in horror. Just the thought of firing one of her people was abhorrent to her.

"Yes."

"Cord, you don't understand. There are reasons he's the way he is." She was more than a little upset and made no effort to hide it. But she knew once she explained, Cord would see he was wrong, would see there was no reason to fire Billy Joe.

"Honey . . ." Cord began more gently. He took his seat across from her once more and leaned forward, his hands clasped loosely between his knees.

"I've seen him throw a wrench halfway across the hangar for no apparent reason. Any problem brought to his attention sets him off. He becomes defensive and downright belligerent. He yelled at Pete last week because Pete found an oil leak in one of the planes Billy Joe supposedly checked. Everyone walks around on egg-

shells because of Billy Joe. That is not the best environ-
ment for a workplace. He's yet another one of your
problems."

Honey's eyes were shining with unshed tears. She
hadn't realized Billy Joe was going through such a hard
time, and she was ashamed. Cord had dominated her
thoughts since his arrival; otherwise, she would have realized Billy Joe needed some special handling and maybe a
friend to talk to.

"I need to talk to him, find out what's wrong. Maybe Evelyn's pregnancy isn't going well. Maybe something is seriously wrong." Her worry and concern for
Billy Joe and his family were evident in her voice and
eyes.

Cord reached up to rub the back of his neck. He shook
his head in disbelief and looked over at Honey with a sad
smile.

"You're too soft for this kind of thing. That's why I
think you need to hire a manager, someone who could
look at this from a business standpoint."

Honey bristled, and her brown eyes shot sparks of re-
newed anger when she looked up.

"You mean someone who wouldn't even take into account the fact that each person is an individual, with special needs, special problems. Well, I won't have it. I'll
have a good business, and happy people. I won't turn my
air show over to someone who doesn't care who works at
the show so long as we make a profit."

"Even if it means no partnership with Wayne and
Cray?" Cord questioned with a raised eyebrow.

Honey froze. Her eyes flew up to clash with his in a
duel she had no hope of winning. She suddenly knew why
he was so well respected in the business world. Cordell
Wayne was not merely a man recovering from his fiancée's death, amusing himself until he decided to return

home to his own business, as she'd heard rumored. He was a consummate businessman, and clashing with this side of him was frightening.

"Will you refuse to invest in my show if I refuse to take on a manager?" she asked, a slight quaver in her voice.

Cord saw her fear, heard it, and was ashamed that he had caused such a reaction in her. He didn't want her to fear him. He didn't want to be the cause of her pain. No matter how right he might be, having Honey afraid of him was intolerable. It hurt.

Cord reached across the space separating them, taking one of her cold hands, which was resting on her thigh, between the warmth of his own palms. He didn't stop to question his actions, he only knew he had to erase the fear from her eyes.

"Honey, I'll teach you what you need to know to manage the airshow effectively," he promised.

Honey felt heat flowing back into her body, radiating up from her hand which he still held. The gentleness of his eyes warmed her more, and her fear began to fade.

"And Billy Joe?" she questioned, needing further reassurance.

"Honey, I have to be honest. I'm going to try to get you to see what a problem he is. Maybe you'll realize I'm right. And in the meantime, I'll see if he gets any better in his attitude. Okay?"

Honey nodded and smiled. This was the Cord she had seen in the tavern and each day at the hangar, the one she knew. He was fair, honest, and, above all, gentle. She had no reason to fear him.

"Thank you, Cord," she murmured.

Cord felt as though the sun had come out. No trace of fear remained in her eyes. All he saw was trust and a growing warmth. He dropped her hand.

"I, uh, better be leaving," he said hoarsely. He'd promised she would be safe with him, and he knew he had to get out of the beach house, now, if he hoped to keep that promise. The way she was looking at him, as if the sun rose and set in him, was enough to test any man's control. In the space of a few moments, everything had changed.

He stood and headed for the door, not even waiting for her to accompany him. He opened the door and turned back to see her walking toward him, a puzzled look in her large doe-soft brown eyes. That damned sweater slipped off her shoulder again.

"I'll see you tomorrow," he said quickly. He stepped outside and closed the door as he heard her respond, "Tomorrow."

Cord gulped in air and just stood there, at the top of the stairs. He heard her lock the door and breathed a sigh of relief. He didn't know what he would have done if she'd opened the door and found him still standing there. Yes, he did. The knowledge of what he would have done haunted him as he headed down the stairs. He had no control around her.

At least he had time now, time to step back and try to stay away from Honey. Tomorrow he'd . . . Cord groaned as he reached for the doorknob on the RV. He had agreed to go up in her Cessna tomorrow. What was even worse was the fact that he needed to see her books, the sooner the better, especially if he planned to give her an answer after her first show.

Whether he wanted to or not, he was going to have to start working closely with Honey. That meant he had to find some way to control himself when he was around her. Easy. About as easy as building and flying an airplane— three hundred years ago.

*   *   *

"Now, Ronnie . . ." Honey began again. Between practice and planning sessions, she'd been trying to get him into a plane throughout the morning. Cord had been busy with Matt and Billy Joe, as he told her yesterday. She was still concerned that Cord was going to keep asking her to fire Billy Joe, but she felt confident she could change his mind, especially after last night when he'd been so gentle with her.

So, this morning after Ronnie had hauled the last of the dispensable garbage from her office, leaving clippings, folders, some trade magazines, and what looked like important papers, behind, she decided it was time to find out what he had against flying. She'd cornered him, trying to get him to take a short flight with her. She wanted to show him how wonderful flying could be. Instead, she was finding you just didn't corner Ronnie.

Ronnie had no intention of going up in a plane, not even with Cord. She'd even tried teasing him into going, but his usual good humor didn't extend to the subject of flying, and he wouldn't tell her why.

"My body ain't gettin' up in that *thing*!"

"It's all perfectly safe," Honey soothed, becoming exasperated by his vehemence. She didn't understand his hostile reaction. Around a plane engine, he was fine, but now that she was trying to lead him into the cabin, he bucked like an unbroken pony.

"If I'd been meant to fly, I'd have long feathered things growin' out of my shoulders!"

Ronnie scowled down at Honey, and she scowled right back at him. Then, her features relaxed with her sudden realization.

"You're afraid," she murmured gently.

"*I am not!* I'm just not stupid enough to go up in that little sardine can with wings."

"It's not little, not a sardine can, and furthermore, it's

safer than driving." Afraid or not, he had no right to talk that way about her plane.

"Tell it to the cameras, but not me!"

"Children, now we mustn't bicker on the runway." Cord was trying hard to suppress his laughter. He'd seen their heated exchange from the hangar as he approached them. He knew Honey, with her love of flying, would eventually try to get Ronnie into a plane, and he also knew she was destined to fail.

"Oh, shut up!" Honey and Ronnie snapped in unison, turning to glare at Cord.

Cord couldn't help it, he laughed, drawing twin growls of rage from the combatants. Shaking his head, he moved to slip one arm around Ronnie's shoulders and the other around Honey's.

"Okay, you two, I take it this is all about flying. The solution's simple. Ronnie, you'll stay here. Honey, you'll go."

"No joke," Ronnie shot back, moving away from them and heading toward the hangar without another word.

Realizing he still held Honey against his side, Cord reluctantly released her and moved away.

"I'll preflight the plane," Honey murmured huskily. She left Cord where he was, but she still felt the effect of his brief touch. It was all well and good to say they would keep things businesslike, but that didn't keep her body from reacting when Cord touched her. She found it much easier to deal with Cord when he *wasn't* touching her.

When she finished checking the plane, she turned to look for Cord, and almost ran into his muscular chest when she found him right behind her.

"Ready?"

"Sure," he replied confidently.

"Then let's go." Honey climbed in and deftly strapped

herself into the pilot's seat, watching as Cord settled himself beside her.

Honey ran through her checklist, opened her window, and shouted "Clear!" before starting the propeller. She then picked up the hand-held microphone, adjusted the radio frequency, and tested her transmission.

Cord sat back and relaxed, taking note of her obvious expertise. But he also saw the restrained excitement in her sparkling eyes at the prospect of taking off, of being able to soar into the air. That same look was in her eyes each time she headed out to take her plane up for a flight. It was one of the reasons he'd questioned her commitment to the airshow. This was what she loved. It was what she was born to do. He'd once thought the same thing about himself, until last year. As they taxied down the apron and lined up for takeoff, Cord experienced a slight surge of panic.

"Why won't Ronnie go up in a plane?" Honey asked as she maneuvered the plane onto the runway.

"He went up once, when he first went to work for me." Cord stopped talking as Honey's concentration returned to the takeoff. He felt the panic easing and took a deep breath, relaxing even more.

The plane surged forward, picking up speed as she pushed in the throttle. As the plane lifted, she quickly made adjustments, murmuring into the mike before easing the plane's rate of climb to a safer angle. Honey never took chances, not unless she'd calculated the odds beforehand, and when she was close to the ground, she was especially careful.

When they reached three thousand feet, Honey leveled off. Turning to Cord, her eyes lit from within, she flashed him a radiant smile, only to find him sprawled comfortably in his seat.

"You okay?"

"Sure."

"So what happened to turn him off flying?" Honey questioned, picking up on their previous conversation.

"The plane had to make an emergency landing. Ronnie walked away without a scratch, but the pilot was pretty banged up. The pilot lived, and Ronnie hasn't gotten in a plane since." Cord shrugged. He knew how frightened Ronnie had been. He also understood why Ronnie chose not to fly. Accidents happened . . .

"That's too bad," Honey murmured with regret. For anyone to not know the joys of flying, to her, was unthinkable.

"You fly well. How long have you been doing it?" Cord questioned, shaking off his bad memories and turning to look out the side window, to the ground far below.

Honey glanced over at him again and found herself feeling inordinately pleased that Cord seemed at ease. He seemed to love flying almost as much as she did.

"I've been flying all my life. Dad was a pilot. He flew anything he could, and a few things they said he couldn't, until he developed the infection that damaged his inner ear. Mom and Dad retired to Glenwood, in the foothills of the Blue Ridge Mountains, close enough to an airfield so Dad can spend time there."

"Was your dad a test pilot?"

"No, not really," she responded, scanning her instrument panel when they hit some turbulence. "He just loved being up here. He felt so free, so alive. The sky was his mistress, my mom used to say."

Cord found himself watching her animated face. If the sky had been her father's mistress, then it was now Honey's consort. She seemed finely tuned to its every nuance. She flowed with the plane, accepting turbulence and wind variance with ease. Her eyes seemed to caress the vast open blueness before her, delighting in the scattered cottonball clouds. No one could ever accuse her of not loving her job. The way she handled the plane, he knew she carried on her own love affair with the sky . . . the way he used to.

It felt right to be up here again. Looking out, he experienced a drowning surge of emotion. It was so eternal, so beautiful. With a start, he suddenly realized how much he'd missed it. It was like coming home again.

"From the file my father sent us, I read you've had the show almost two years now." Cord turned to watch her response. Last night, he'd learned why she kept the show, now he wanted to hear the history. He needed to hear it from her. But more than that, he wanted to watch her, to hear her soft, sexy voice, to touch her.

"Yes. My husband had the dream of a multifaceted airshow, offering everything, including stunt flying for movies if they were shooting out here. We struggled along for about three years, borrowing planes, putting on small, quality shows. Then his plane went down during a show. He was doing a power dive off a double loop, and his plane went into the runway. He died instantly."

"You loved him," Cord stated, having read the emotions crossing her face.

"Yes. Very much. We met at an airfield outside of Norfolk, Virginia, five years ago. We fell in love, and we married. Sometimes I still miss him, but I cherish the memory of the time we had together. I know he's at peace." A fond smile of remembrance curved her lips, and she failed to notice the sudden rigidity of Cord's body.

"Weren't you angry?" he rasped, memories of his own making his voice harsh.

Startled, Honey's glance took in his emotionless expression, the control he seemed to be exerting. "Yes," she replied honestly, sensing his need to know and understand.

"I was angry, numb, bewildered, shocked, hurt, saddened, and hysterical—everything any other person would have been at such a loss. Eventually it passed, and now I remember the good times, without anger.''

"You sure don't seem to be dwelling on it or pining over his death," Cord drawled insultingly. He knew it wasn't fair the minute he said it.

"Andy wouldn't have wanted me to ram into a tree to follow him. Nor would he have wanted me to stop living in any *other* way. He's gone, and I was left behind. I accepted that a long time ago. Having the airshow has helped, and I love it. It's a constant challenge.''

"Doesn't it remind you of his death? Aren't you afraid?" Cord questioned more normally.

"Yes, there is a reminder here," Honey admitted. Her eyes were trained on her instruments, and she wouldn't look at Cord. "The reminder is that if you make mistakes, you don't walk away. But in order to go on in this business, my men and I have to believe it won't happen to us.''

"But it could," Cord continued stubbornly.

"No. I'm better than that, and I'm careful. It won't happen to me.''

"Don't the aerobatics bother you?"

"I don't fly aerobatic demonstrations in the shows," she admitted.

"Did you before the accident?"

"Yes. I enjoy flying them, I always have. But now, I won't perform near the runway. I fly for my own pleasure, and for the satisfaction of doing the maneuvers correctly.''

"Why didn't you change professions?"

Honey looked at him as if he was crazy.

"Cord, I love what I do. I've been flying my whole life, with my dad before I could even walk, on my own as soon as I was old enough. When you find a job you love, and get paid doing it, you'd be crazy to walk away.

People get killed crossing the street and taking a shower. Do you stop doing those things because of that?''

"No." Lord, she made it sound so reasonable, so easy. But he knew it wasn't that easy, not always.

"So how often do you fly for pleasure?" Cord questioned, changing the subject.

"Not as often as I'd like." Honey laughed, the sound musical and pleasing as it filled the small cabin.

"Are you up to some rolls and loops?" Cord questioned, trying to make up for his earlier comments. He knew it wasn't her fault that the memories of Gina still hurt so much.

Honey took up the challenge, and her gentle smile made Cord ache. He smiled back, and his earlier anger was forgotten. Now, there was only Honey and the beauty of the sky spread out before them. They climbed higher after she picked up the mike and announced her intention to practice.

Suddenly, Honey felt very much alive, as if talking about Andy had freed her. She'd felt the same way last night, when Cord had made her see the show as hers, as her dream now. Maybe she was just being fanciful, but she sensed that Cord needed the same kind of release. Perhaps he needed to talk about his fiancée, and when he was ready, she planned to be there for him. Mentally, Honey shrugged her shoulders and stopped thinking about the past or future. She just wanted to enjoy this time in the air . . . with Cord.

"Hang on," she called in warning.

Honey made a deft move, and suddenly Cord found himself looking up at a green-and-yellow sky and down at a deep-blue ground with puffy white mountains as the plane did a four-point roll. After leveling off and increasing speed, she pulled back on the joystick and began a simple loop. Coming out of the loop, another move had the plane rolling as though avoiding enemy fire, like the original barnstormers of old.

Cord's chuckle blended with her delighted laughter and rang through the cabin. "You're not prone to air sickness, are you?" she finally asked.

"Not a bit," Cord returned, glad his stomach was like cast iron, and hoping it wouldn't choose this moment to prove him a liar.

"Want to take over for a few?" Honey questioned, righting the plane once again. She knew he wasn't stupid enough to take the controls if he wasn't up to flying. That wasn't his style.

"Yes, I think I would." Placing his hands on the controls, Cord let himself get the "feel" of the plane before trying anything. His medical wasn't current, and technically, he knew he shouldn't be flying without a current exam. But he wanted to try it. He wanted to fly again. Within minutes, it had all come back, and like riding a bicycle, he was flying with much of his old expertise.

With a deft twist, he turned the plane into a slow loop, gracefully soaring through the sky.

"It handles well," he remarked innocently, turning to glance at Honey once he'd righted the plane.

Serenely calm, Honey just smiled and murmured, "Yes, she does." Knowing Cord knew his way around an airplane pleased her. She knew he hadn't flown in at least a year, and she expected his skills to be a little rusty, but Cord had the graceful, competent, and coordinated movements of a seasoned pilot. There was no awkwardness. His every move shouted confidence in his ability to handle the plane. She watched his strong hands almost caress the controls, saw the intensity of his gaze on the instruments, and a longing to have his hands on her again caused her to catch her breath sharply. To cover her sudden, unguarded desire, Honey smiled brightly, averting her eyes from any chance glance he might give her. She looked out the window until she had composed herself once more.

"You're not bad," she finally commented, facing Cord who was turning toward the airfield and beginning his descent.

"I improve as time passes."

"You mean like wine?"

Cord chuckled, turning the Cessna for its final approach. He spoke into the mike and announced his position. Since Honey's airfield didn't have a tower, it was up to the pilot to keep watch and to announce his intentions.

Honey's faith in him as he took the controls still disturbed him, but he was oddly pleased as well. She'd sat calmly, not trying to grab the controls when he sent them plummeting toward the ground. She had trusted his skill, having known little about his experience, having lost her husband in an airshow accident. It was disconcerting. Either she was very sure of her ability to recover from his error or she was an especially trusting, and, therefore, totally dangerous, woman. But of course, he already knew just how dangerous she was, at least to him.

"Are all the pilots as good as you?"

"Yes," Honey stated with pride. Charlie Phesner, a slimeball and her major competitor, had a bigger show. But she had quality flyers and jumpers who were just as talented as his.

Honey watched Cord's every movement in preparation for their landing. Not only did most accidents occur on takeoff and landings, but the true test of a pilot was how smoothly and efficiently he could accomplish both feats. When they touched down and the scenery began speeding past, Honey smiled to herself. Cord *was* good. In fact, as a pilot, he was excellent. The touchdown, sometimes a jarring experience with certain pilots, had been like a feather floating down to settle on a tabletop.

After completing the postflight check, Honey and Cord walked side by side toward the hangar.

"So what do you want to do now?" she questioned.

"See your books."

SEVEN

Seeing her books was not a good idea. He knew it. It meant being alone with Honey, locked away in her office, just the two of them.

There was no one left to use as a buffer between them, no other valid task he could do. He'd talked to, and worked with, the men. He understood how the show was run. He even understood some of the basic problems. He hadn't lied to Honey last night when he said he had seen the potential in her airshow. Now, the only thing left was for him to go over her financial and business records. He had no choice but to work with Honey.

He had thought Ronnie might still be there, cleaning up. But Ronnie was gone, heaven only knew where. From the looks of things, Ronnie had managed to clear away a lot of the accumulated junk. But the desk, and every other surface, was still piled with the things Honey had to go through.

Cord practically groaned as Honey bent over from the waist to sift through a stack of files on the floor in front of her desk. From his position, leaning against the closed door, he had a most gratifying view of her perfectly shaped behind.

"Dammit, Honey, don't you know where your books are?" he snapped in frustration.

Honey jumped and spun to face him, her dark-brown eyes wide with hurt feelings.

"No, Cord, I don't. You've known all along how this office looks. Why are you jumping on me now? I *am* trying to find them, you know?"

"Sorry." Cord closed his eyes as she turned back to search through more papers.

Now he knew how soft-hearted hunters felt. It was like shooting Bambi. But what did she expect him to do when she flaunted herself in front of him?

He was being a jackass and he knew it. How was she supposed to know that just seeing her walk across the hangar was enough to raise his blood pressure to a dangerous level? She was just being herself. It wasn't her fault he couldn't control his own body. Maybe he should have waited until tomorrow, until he had a chance to distance himself from her.

Cord opened his eyes, only to find her across the room, her arms over her head as she pulled some files from the top of the filing cabinet. From the side, that position showed the high curve of her breasts. Cord bit the inside of his bottom lip. He could still feel the way her breast fit his hand, could still taste her on his tongue.

Honey tugged on the stubborn files once more. She felt the tall stack moving, and suddenly she was struggling to keep them from falling. As they began to topple toward her head, Cord's strong hands grabbed her shoulders and pulled her out of the way.

Honey watched the files, and a few large books, hit the floor where she had been standing moments ago. With a sigh, she leaned back against Cord's body.

"I . . . Thanks, Cord," she said, a rasp of fear threading her voice. She knew she could have been injured. At that moment, she wanted nothing more than to turn into the safety of his arms.

"N-no problem" came his husky reply. Still, he didn't release her.

When she heard the catch in his voice and felt the trembling of his hands, something changed inside her. She knew he wanted her to turn around, to bring their bodies together. Instinctively, she obeyed his silent desire. Slowly, she turned to face him, wrapping her arms around him and laying her head against his broad chest.

Cord stiffened, his hands falling loosely to his sides. Then, as though he was no longer in control, his hands raised to rest on her back, holding her against him. He could feel her breasts against his chest, her silken arms tight about his waist, her head snuggled under his chin.

He could smell the clean, outdoor freshness of her perfume mixed with her own subtle scent, and he heard the gentle rhythm of her breath, felt her movements against him. It was only the third time he'd held her, and yet it felt right. His body knew she was perfect. A year was a long time to be without the closeness of a woman, without the closeness of anyone. It was too long, much too long . . .

"Honey," Cord breathed, lifting her face with one of his fingers under her chin.

Honey's eyes met his, and her lips parted in silent invitation. When his lips were a heartbeat away from hers, he stopped. He watched her lashes flutter closed in anticipation of his touch, and he knew he was lost. He wanted to stop, needed to stop, but there was a part of him, a much stronger part that wanted to go on, to again know the honeyed warmth of her mouth. His will surrendered to the stronger desire. Once more, his reason deserted him. There was only Honey, only this moment.

Honey's hands slid down his sides, sweeping up his

chest to clasp around his neck. Shifting, she pressed closer, wanting to feel him against her pliant body, reveling in the sensuous contact, wanting more. Gently, she brushed his lower lip with the tip of her tongue.

Cord answered her sexy request, parting his lips for her. With a purring murmur, he allowed her to deepen the kiss, and his hands slid to her rounded bottom, pulling her up to fit intimately against his strength. Cord felt her breath catch at the contact, could feel the trembling of her breasts before she sighed against his mouth.

Honey's hands slid higher, plunging into Cord's thick, vibrant hair. She moved against his aroused body.

"Cord . . ." Honey's voice whispered across his ears as she pulled back, focusing on him, needing to see his face, to know what he was feeling. She saw the golden fire of passion in his eyes, the heavy sensuality of desire in his face, and she trembled. Her breasts peaked in arousal. Her thighs quivered in longing.

Why was she so attracted to this man? Why was her body responding this way, as it never had before she met Cord? Why?

Cord didn't want to question the why's. He only knew that after a year of being with women who left him cold, he was with a woman he desired, more than even he had thought possible. Their first kiss had been a mere prelude. The embrace last night had been a teasing glimpse of heaven. Now, his body strained for release. He couldn't think clearly with Honey in his arms. He only knew he wanted her, needed her. Now.

He captured her intoxicating mouth, silencing her. With his hands still cupping her soft bottom, Cord lifted her and backed her against the dark, wood-paneled wall. He felt her small hands lock behind his neck for leverage, and a moan rumbled low in his throat.

Running his palms down her thighs, he pulled her legs

around his hips and stepped even closer, his arousal nestling against her trembling softness, moving rhythmically, showering them both with images of what would happen if their clothing no longer separated them.

With his hands free, he could touch her the way he longed to, could touch every seductive, beautifully sensuous inch of her. His lips still held hers captive, his tongue probing in rhythm with his pulsating body.

Honey moaned deep in her throat, unable to resist his magic. Her mind shut down and her body continued to respond, to revel in Cord's mastery of it.

Caressing and gently kneading her thighs, Cord's hands traversed from her knees to her hips, sliding to her slender waist. His hands trembled on finding the underside of her breasts through the material of her coverall. As he cupped the overflowing softness of her breasts, he felt the aroused peaks pressing against his palms. Reluctantly leaving her lips, his hungry mouth found her neck, nipping at the taut skin below her ear. Hearing her cry, he jerked his head away in surprise. His hands moved to her waist, supporting her, fearing he had hurt her.

"Honey, wha—?"

"Cord! Cord . . . please . . ." Honey gasped, unable to slow the fast pace of her heart or her deep, uneven breathing. She knew they had to stop, knew they were going too fast. This wasn't right.

"Please *what*?" Cord rasped, pressing brief, rough kisses along her jaw when he realized she wasn't hurt. His breath came short and harsh from his throat, matching her own pants.

"Please sto— Ohhh," Honey moaned when Cord nipped at the sensitive spot below her ear once more.

Honey's hands quickly captured his face between her palms. If she allowed him to continue, she'd lose all reason. In response, he took her soft, kiss-swollen lips once again, gently thrusting his hips against her in a deeply disturbing motion.

"I need you, Honey. Please, I need you," Cord gasped against her mouth, his hands working at the zipper of her coverall, his hips bracing her against the wall. He lowered his head to search for the treasure he was uncovering, and didn't see the tears that slipped from her eyes.

Cord tasted the hollow of her throat while his hands worked the zipper down, exposing more of her breasts. As he returned to her lips, his cheek brushed her own, feeling the inexplicable wetness there. Experimentally, his tongue ran over her smooth, velvety skin, tasting the saltiness of her tears. He felt her tremble in reaction to his exploratory lick, and confusion dulled the raging, passionate heat of his body.

Opening his eyes, Cord saw the tears trailing down her cheeks to her chin, where they dripped onto the creamy lushness of her quivering breasts. Retracing their path, he found her eyes tightly closed and her thick lashes matted together by the salty wetness seeping from the corners. His passion dulled even further, concern for her taking precedence.

"Honey? Honey, tell me what's wrong. Did I hurt you?" Cord questioned, his voice still husky with passion. Desperately, he tried to gain control. The fire in his blood was fierce, but he couldn't quench it at Honey's expense. He couldn't hurt her just to ease the ache in his body.

When Honey refused to look at him and shook her head, fresh tears trailed over her cheeks. Cord's sweeping gaze found what looked like a chair behind the desk, under a mass of papers. Holding Honey around her waist to support her, he stepped away from the wall and felt the uncomfortable tightness of his jeans. Lifting her into his arms, he tilted the accumulated junk off the chair before sitting down and gingerly setting her on his lap. He pulled her against his chest and rocked slowly. Once more, her tears were doing something to him, touching parts of him he had thought long dead.

"What's wrong, Honey? How did I hurt you?" Cord crooned. Images of what he'd just done to her started to flash through his mind. Shame at his behavior quickly followed. He had thought he could handle being alone with her. Obviously he was wrong.

Honey hiccupped, completely mortified. She couldn't abide women who continually burst into tears. Her arms were still wrapped around his neck, and she buried her face between her arm and his shoulder.

"I'm sorry, Cord," she mumbled.

"For what?" he asked, surprised by her apology. He was the one who owed *her* an apology.

"Icagthit" came the muffled reply.

"English, please," Cord chuckled, and was amazed that she could make him laugh after what had just happened.

"I . . ." Honey sniffed, facing him, bracing herself for his anger. She pulled her arms away from him and clasped her hands between her thighs. "I can't go through with it."

"What?"

"*It.*"

"Trust me. I already figured that out."

Cord's rueful tone surprised her. She had expected his anger and frustration. She'd made no effort to stop him, had even welcomed his advances. She was torn between her desire for Cord and her belief in love being a very basic, and necessary, prerequisite to making love. Honey knew she had no right to lead Cord on. It wasn't fair to him.

"I shouldn't have . . . well . . ." Honey began in confusion.

"Shouldn't have what?" Cord asked gently.

"You know, led you on . . ."

"Honey, you didn't lead me anywhere. I galloped right along, all on my own."

"But . . ."

"Hush, Honey, you have nothing to apologize for. I should be the one to apologize." Cord cradled her head under his chin, beginning to rock her once again. His arms still held her close, in spite of her rigid posture.

"Thank you, Cord." Honey relaxed against him, sighing in contentment. She laid her head against his shoulder and lifted one hand to place it on the center of his chest.

"For what?"

"For being so nice about all this. I didn't expect . . . Well, we just seem to . . . and I didn't mean to . . ."

"It wasn't your fault. We both know what happens when we get together."

"I know, and you should want to kill me right now." She still couldn't bring herself to look at him. But she was enjoying the safety and security of his strong arms, even though she knew she should move away from him.

"There are things I'd like to do to you, with you, but killing's not one of them."

"Oh."

"Oh, indeed." Cord chuckled.

Honey pushed away from his chest and looked up into his eyes. "Are you all right?"

Cord stiffened. Her concern was like a punch in his solar plexus, bringing it all back, all the reasons he had no business here, with her, like this. He could have accepted her teasing, her laughter, or even her discomfort. He couldn't accept her concern. He didn't deserve it.

"I'll be fine," he grated. He stood abruptly, almost tossing her from his lap. Without a backward glance, he strode out of the room.

Honey leaned against the desk and stared at the closed door in confused dismay. What had she done?

There was no way she could deny what she was feeling for Cord. She was attracted to him in a way she'd never been attracted to another man. The more she came to know him, the more she liked and respected him. What she felt for Cord wasn't the same thing she had felt for her husband. This was stronger, deeper, and very different. She couldn't ignore her responses to Cord. Each time he touched her, she melted. Yet she couldn't ignore her belief in love, commitment, forever. So where did that leave them?

With a sigh, Honey became aware of an uncomfortable moisture between her breasts. She reached up to wipe away the results of her tears with the faded khaki material of her coveralls, and found naked skin. Looking down, she saw her breasts were almost bare and small marks were beginning to form on her creamy skin. She collapsed onto the chair she and Cord had shared and pulled up the zipper to cover her bareness.

When the office door opened, she looked up expectantly, over the smaller stack of papers on her desk. Her hope died as she saw Ronnie standing there. His lopsided smile of greeting quickly faded as he took in her appearance. She was embarrassed for Ronnie to catch her in this condition, again. Once more, she knew she must look terrible. Her hair was coming out of its braid, her coverall was rumpled and wrinkled, and bunched in embarrassing places. She knew her lips were swollen and must be red and tender-looking, and there was no way she could hide her red eyes or the tears that were drying on her cheeks. Without a word, he turned away, but not before she saw the thundering rage flash across his suddenly old face.

*   *   *

"Cord! Cord, where the hell are you?!"

"In the shower, where the hell do you think?" Cord shot back, trying to ease the ache in his body and blank his mind. He had come a long way this last year, even longer in the last month. He was starting to believe he could go home again. But he wasn't ready to get tangled up with another woman, no matter what his body thought. In his mind it would be disloyal to Gina's memory, especially after the way he had treated her. Already he was feeling twinges of guilt for what had taken place in Honey's office. Last night had been bad enough, but to almost take Honey against the wall of her office . . . How could he have lost control that way?

"I want to talk to you!" Ronnie yelled.

"I'm coming." Pulling on his jeans, and thankful they weren't as uncomfortable as they had been before, Cord sauntered out of the small cubicle into the cramped hall of the RV. "So what's so . . . ?"

Cord's voice trailed off. He saw Ronnie standing billboard straight not six feet from him. The younger man's fists were held rigidly at his sides, trembling, ready to lash out.

Warily, Cord tossed his towel around his shoulders to absorb the dripping water from his hair.

"What's up?"

"You made her cry," Ronnie spat in accusation.

"She's all right." Cord shrugged, realizing Ronnie must have seen Honey and come looking for him.

"If you call looking as though she's been laid 'all right.' "

"Ronnie," Cord rumbled in warning.

"What's the matter, Big Man? Finally had to *prove* you were a man." Ronnie's entire body was shaking with the force of his outrage.

DETACH AND MAIL CARD TODAY—

FIRST CLASS
MAIL

OFFICIAL ENTRY CARD

Kismet Romances
"$1,000,000+ Sweepstakes"
PO Box 7249
PHILA PA 19101-9895

PLACE
POSTAGE
STAMP
HERE

"What's got into you? You didn't say one word last night, and let's face it, there've been times you've practically thrown women at me."

Cord couldn't believe Ronnie's reaction. Ronnie had never been out of control, at least not in the years Cord had known him. Ronnie was street-wise, tough, sarcastic, grudgingly friendly, and even sensitive at times, but never, ever out of control.

"Last night she didn't cry. Besides, you knew what kind of women those other ones were," Ronnie ground out.

"Yes, I knew. What's to say this one's any different?" Cord knew his words were born of guilt and frustration, and he wanted to recall them immediately.

Before he could retract his statement, Ronnie sprang without warning. Cord saw the punch in time to lessen its impact, but not divert it. Ronnie's fist landed squarely on his jaw, and he jerked away. Cord sprawled the length of the hall, looking up at Ronnie in disbelief.

Ronnie had hit him! Cord couldn't believe Ronnie had actually hit him.

Apparently Ronnie couldn't believe it, either, because he turned a strange shade of green as he stared down at Cord in shock. He absently rubbed his knuckles, and in a less angry voice than before, continued. "She's different. You know it, and that's why you been duckin' her for most of the past month. It's why you're saying what you don't mean. Hell, that's why she turns you on to begin with."

Cord sat up slowly, leaned against the paneled wall and tested his jaw. If the full force had landed, he was sure it would have been fractured. For his size, Ronnie packed a heck of a lot of power behind his punch. Slowly, warily, Cord stood. He still said nothing, just continued to watch Ronnie, and listen.

"I've watched you for years, Cord. I saw you with Gina, and even *I* could see the love you both had. But since she died, any woman you've met, any woman you could have been serious about, any really nice woman, you ran away from, or you drove her away."

"Ron . . ."

"Shut up! I'm real tired of hearing your voice. You never say nothin' important, not anymore. So now, you're gonna listen." Ronnie's initial anger was fading, and his voice had lowered.

"All right." Cord walked around Ronnie to sit on one of the chairs in the living room of the RV. Ronnie followed and leaned back against the kitchen counter, pushing his hands into the back pockets of his tight jeans.

"You been runnin' for months now. In the beginning, I could understand. You was hurtin'. Hell, even I would'a run. But you're still runnin'. People got to take chances in life in order to be living. You aren't living. You exist. You try passing out money to feel alive, but it doesn't help, does it? It never has," Ronnie muttered sadly.

Cord was silent, stunned to hear Ronnie, of all people, saying these things.

"Gina's dead, Cord. She's been dead for over a year. But you're alive, man. You didn't die with her. You might wish you had, but you didn't. She wouldn't want this, would she?" Ronnie looked up to face Cord this time.

"Honey's a lady, a real lady. Maybe she reminds you of Gina, but dammit, it's not her fault. You didn't have to . . ." Ronnie hesitated, searching for the right words. "Grow up, man! I'm not saying you should forget Gina, but maybe it's time you let her go. How do you expect to help anybody else if you can't even help yourself?"

"Ron . . ." Cord began.

"What?" Ronnie snapped.

"Ron, I didn't. I swear I didn't. I didn't hurt Honey,

not that way. I couldn't. She cried because she felt bad about not . . . Why the devil do you think I was in the shower, a cold shower, in the middle of the day?'' Cord finally questioned, his voice gruff.

Ronnie's face cleared before the cocky, self-assured mask dropped back into place. "I didn't think about it," he said honestly.

"Think about it next time okay? I don't need another right cross. And speaking of right crosses, the next time you pull that stunt, I won't just accept it like I did today, if you get my meaning." Cord's voice was a growl of warning, but a rueful smile curved his lips.

"Yeah, I got you," Ronnie replied as he dropped onto the couch opposite Cord.

"Cried because she couldn't, huh?" Ronnie questioned after a moment.

Uncomfortably, Cord grunted an affirmative response.

"Damn! I'd like to find me a woman like that," Ronnie said almost to himself, a wistfulness lighting his features.

"What?" Cord rasped in surprise. The idea that self-assured, lust-'em-and-leave-'em Ronnie was looking for a special woman was something he'd never considered.

"You got a problem with that?" Ronnie growled defensively.

"No, not me." Cord hid a smile as he stood up. He moved into the kitchen and pulled a couple of sodas out of the refrigerator. Tossing one to Ronnie, Cord leaned back against the kitchen counter to open his.

His mind went to Honey, beautiful, sexy Honey. She'd been so concerned about him after the way he'd almost taken her against the wall of her office. And he'd rebelled against that concern. He was a selfish bastard. The one time he had tried to be noble, everything had fallen apart. Yes, Honey was something all right; he just wished he could figure out what. Maybe he needed to get away for a while.

Lord, was Ronnie right about him? Just what was he running from? Memories? He didn't know anymore.

Shaking his head, Cord thought over the past month. For the first time since her death he hadn't been constantly remembering Gina, or rather, fighting *not* to remember. He'd been able to laugh, to honestly enjoy what he was doing instead of just doing what was expected. Trying to keep things "strictly business" with Honey hadn't worked. When he was with her . . . But that was something he would deal with later, much later.

For now, how did he salvage the situation?

What was he going to do about the Johnson Airshow? What was he going to do the next time he saw Honey? For that matter, what was *she* going to do?

EIGHT

Honey sighed as she locked the hangar and turned to stare at the motor home that had been absent for the past week, since the day Cord had left her in her office. Only the note taped to her Cessna had assured her they would be back. It hadn't helped.

Tomorrow, the first weekend of May, was their first show, the start of their summer season. The Johnson Airshow had contracts through September, at least one show per month, sometimes two. They would be putting on shows in the area, and some as far up as Virginia. If only there was more money, they could travel farther, maybe even increase their show season. But that would come later . . . if it came at all. In order to be a success next year, the planning had to start this year. And everything hinged on Cord. Without him, the Johnson Airshow might not exist next year. It didn't look good.

She had taken the time to talk to Billy Joe while Cord was gone. He'd said he'd try to do better, but he wouldn't tell her what the problem was. She didn't know what Cord was going to demand if he agreed to the partnership. She couldn't get rid of Billy Joe, not when he was so obviously hurting and upset. He needed his job. She knew the other guys at the show were as much Billy Joe's family as they were hers. There had to be a middle ground, something less than firing but more than just ignoring Billy Joe's attitude and disruptions.

Honey sighed again. At least Cord was back. She had missed him the past few days. She had even missed Ronnie. She hadn't realized how much she enjoyed their company, or how much fun it had been since they'd come to the show. Ronnie's teasing always kept her on her toes and made her laugh, and Cord's gentle, quiet strength was like a protective blanket she could snuggle up in. And then there was the fire, the tingling heat Cord's mere presence could elicit within her.

With a shake of her head, Honey walked away from the hangar. If she continued thinking of that she'd never be able to ask for the favor she needed. She only hoped her first meeting with Cord wasn't too awkward. If Billy Joe had thought to leave her some transportation, she could have avoided seeing Cord until after the show. It was already getting dark, Billy Joe still hadn't returned, and she needed to get home.

Reaching the RV, Honey braced herself and rapped softly against the aluminum door.

"Hang on," yelled a muffled voice from inside.

Honey waited patiently. She saw a new crunch on the right rear bumper, smiled, and shook her head. When the door opened and she came face-to-face with Ronnie, she was relieved. Perhaps this favor wouldn't be so hard after all.

"Um . . . Ronnie, I hate to ask, but could you give me a ride home? The guys took the van to a hot-air balloon exhibit. Last year's winners of the Statesville National Balloon Rally are there. Anyway, the guys wanted to meet them and see the people who will be participating in tomorrow's show. My problem is they forgot to leave me some transportation. I'm stranded."

Pure mischief lit Ronnie's bright blue eyes, and Honey frowned, watching him warily.

"No problem. Come on in."

"Thanks," Honey replied as she entered and closed the door behind her.

"Want some coffee?"

"Sure." Coffee was safe enough. "Where's Cord?"

"Asleep in back. He insisted on driving for the past few days. Got a little tired today," Ronnie explained cordially, fixing the coffee while they talked.

Honey stepped into the living-room area and looked around the inside of the RV with undisguised curiosity. It was the first time she'd ventured into Cord and Ronnie's home on wheels. It really was cute and cozy. The furniture was all in shades of brown and beige, and obviously well-worn. It seemed the RV had all the comforts of home—a small television, mobile phone, real plants, and . . . half-naked females? There were pictures of half-naked women all around the loft bed!

"Whose . . . ?" Her high-pitched squeak sounded like she had small furry relatives in the mouse family. Taking a breath, she tried again. "Whose . . . umm, pictures are those?" That was better. At least she *sounded* normal.

Ronnie glanced over his shoulder. "Oh, those are mine."

"I see." Inspecting one closely—well, as close as she could get without being obvious—she wrinkled her nose in distaste. She couldn't help the comment that slipped out.

"Don't you know the sum total of this woman's I.Q. is probably contained in her bra size?"

Turning to Ronnie, Honey found his eyes resting on her

own anatomy. Then, he glanced at one of the pictures in the loft before returning his gaze to her.

"Careful, half-pint, those comments come home to roost, you know."

Honey turned bright red.

"Besides," Ronnie chuckled wickedly, "since talking wasn't on my mind when I put that picture up, I don't figure it matters much."

Honey gulped, trying to compose herself before she either walked home or burst out laughing. "How about some of that coffee I smell? At least then I could put something more tasty in my mouth besides my foot." Sinking onto a seat at the dinette, she was pleased when Ronnie chuckled with her.

"Sure thing."

Honey lazed back against the brown plaid cushion, closed her eyes, and relaxed. It had been a long day, and when Cord saw the new accumulation of junk in her office, he was going to pitch a fit. But at least she had found her books, and the records he wanted to look over.

"Coffee's on," Ronnie drawled, and she heard a thunk on the table in front of her.

Opening her eyes, she reached for the coffee. Her hand froze in midair. Sitting before her was a "mammary mug." She knew what it was because she had seen one in the novelty store at the mall in Nags Head. A twin to it sat across from her, cupped now rather firmly in Ronnie's large palm. Looking up, she found his sparkling eyes surveying her every move, waiting.

"Is this some kind of test?" she questioned, her voice merely curious.

"If it was, you'd be passin'," Ronnie returned with a smile.

"Scamp!" Honey exclaimed in mock reproof before she began to laugh with him.

She couldn't help but find Ronnie's jokes, and his guarded friendship, both infectious and challenging. In the short time she had known him, she felt she finally understood what it was to have a younger brother, a mischievous younger brother to be sure, but that was part of his charm.

"If you do anything except drink your coffee in the proper manner, I'll pour the contents of my mug into your lap and probably ruin any hopes you might have for a family."

Nodding in understanding, Ronnie sipped his coffee and tried to hide his grin.

"Where did you meet Cord, Ronnie?" In the past week, she had grown more and more curious about them. As she and Ronnie sat at the table, sipping coffee, it seemed the perfect time to have her questions answered.

Ronnie chuckled, and a blush spread over his lean cheeks. "He caught me tryin' to steal his car."

"What'd he do?" Honey asked in surprise.

"Gave me a job," Ronnie returned with a disbelieving laugh.

"At his airfield?"

"Yeah. That was, Jeez, six years ago I think. He's a pretty great guy, you know?"

"Yes. He's pretty special," Honey murmured softly, thinking of Cord.

"I'll tell you something he never will, but you can't let on you know. He'd be real uncomfortable about it," Ronnie began in a low tone, his eyes meeting Honey's in all seriousness.

"What?" She had a feeling he was setting her up, but when he continued in the same serious vein, she knew he wasn't.

"When he gave me the job, I was fifteen and a dropout. My old man drank, and I was runnin' with street gangs. Well, Cord found out about my old man; he wasn't nice when he hit the bottle. One day, after I came in with a shiner that 'bout closed my eye, Cord asked me what happened. I wasn't gonna tell him. My old man was a bastard, but I didn't have no one else. Anyway, he kept watch on me. The next time it happened, he went to see my old man, and you know what he did?'' Ronnie's eyes shone with the memory, and his admiration for Cord came through in his voice.

"What?"

"He punched him right in the mouth, told him the next time he hit me, he'd go to jail. 'Course, I never went back there after that. Cord gave me a choice. He said I could go back if I wanted, but he'd give me a room at the airfield if I wanted to live on my own. I was sixteen by then and I stayed at the airfield,'' Ronnie concluded. He took a sip of coffee, not meeting her eyes.

"Sounds to me like Cord is one heck of a guy." Honey's voice was gentle. Ronnie seemed to be uncomfortable now that he'd revealed his past. He couldn't know how much she admired him for what he'd made of himself, and he couldn't know the emotion swelling in her chest at the thought of Cord giving Ronnie such a chance.

"He sure is," Ronnie agreed, still without looking up.

"Ronnie, can you tell me about his fiancée?" Honey knew it wasn't fair to question Ronnie, but she had to have answers so she could understand Cord, and oddly enough, understanding Cord was fast becoming her number-one priority.

"Well, Gina was Tony's daughter. She was sweet, beautiful, kind, and she died last year in a plane crash during a bad storm," Ronnie returned with a self-conscious shrug.

"Cord must have loved her very much."

"Yeah. They loved each other all right. It was like you

read in books, only it wasn't the happy-endin' kind. After she died, he started running, and he ain't stopped yet. To this day, he hates storms. And the only reason he's at your show is 'cause his dad and me tricked him.'' Ronnie shook his head and settled more comfortably onto the bench seat.

"Do *you* know what he's running from?" Sometimes, she'd sensed the same thing in Cord, only she hadn't known the right word to use. He backed away whenever she got too close. And in the beginning, he hadn't wanted to look at her show at all. At least now she understood why.

"Nope. He never talked to me about it. But somethin's sure eatin' at him. Sometimes, when . . . Never mind.'' Ronnie clamped his mouth shut and looked away.

Honey could feel his discomfort, and she could only imagine he was feeling disloyal. It took a special man to foster such loyalty, or to cultivate a friendship with a rebellious teenager and turn him into a responsible adult.

"I'm sorry, Ronnie. Please don't feel I was asking just to gossip. I . . . care about Cord, quite a lot. But he hasn't really talked much about his past, and I have a feeling it's the reason he keeps pulling away, *running*, if you will. I'm just trying to figure him out.''

"That's okay, Honey. I understand, maybe more than you know,'' came his cryptic reply as he stood to clear the table and clean up the kitchenette. Then, he settled into the driver's seat and started the RV's powerful engine.

"Half-pint, could you wake Cord? He hates it when I move the RV and don't tell him, says it bugs him.''

"Okay,'' Honey replied easily. She stood up to do as he asked, and then she paused. Warily, she studied Ronnie's innocent face. Since he probably hadn't even been *born* innocent, she became suspicious. But when he continued to concentrate on the dials and switches on the dash, she shrugged and turned away to do as he asked.

Cautiously, Honey opened the sliding partition to the back bedroom.

"Cord," she called.

She was ready to call out to Cord again, but she wasn't ready when the motor home jerked forward. She catapulted into the shadowy room and sprawled across the queen-size bed and the solid form occupying it.

Cord sprang to a sitting position, disoriented by the warm body lying across his thighs, wriggling and struggling to get up.

"I'm going to kill you, Ronnie," Honey grumbled, all her wonderful thoughts about him turning to murderous ones.

Recognizing the voice, Cord chuckled and reached under her arms, dragging her up to sit beside him. He then plumped his pillow and leaned back on his side, facing her.

"So what are you doing in my bed, Goldilocks?" Cord shifted again to rest his head on one palm, his pillow tucked under his arm. In the half-light provided by the passing streetlamps, he could just make out her expression. She sat in wide-eyed amazement as she stared at him.

Her expression alone was enough to make Cord feel ten feet tall. No woman had ever stared at him with such wonder and curiosity. In the past week, he had imagined what their next meeting would be like, especially after the explosiveness of their last one. But he never imagined this.

In the past few days, while he and Ronnie toured some of the other shows along the coast, he'd thought of her often. The usual result of such thoughts required a cold shower.

One good thing had come from his time away from Honey. He no longer felt guilty for wanting her. He was a man, and he had realized he had his entire life ahead of him. Not only was it ridiculous for him to deny the needs of his body, it was also the height of stupidity to think that he could.

Honey couldn't answer his question. In fact, there wasn't much she *could* do at the moment. Her widened eyes were too busy taking in the sight of Cord's bare chest. His beautiful, broad, bare chest. She had thought she memorized it the day he arrived, but her memory hadn't done him justice.

He was magnificent, firmly muscled, but leanly and subtly so, with a fine mat of curling hair that arrowed down his chest and stopped at the sheet. Seeing his delineated abdominal muscles made her ball her hands into fists to keep from reaching out to trace them with her fingers.

"Earth to Honey," Cord chuckled, waving a hand in front of her eyes to get her attention.

"Oh! Uh, what did you say?" Honey flushed guiltily, glad of the shadows surrounding them in the darkened room.

"What are you doing in my bed?"

"Ronnie, the low-down, double-dealing, tricky rat, told me to tell you he was taking me home," Honey explained.

"I beg your pardon?"

"I said—"

"Never mind," Cord interrupted softly. "Ronnie, why are we taking Honey home, and why's she back here?" he called out.

"Doesn't have a car, and I sent her."

"Thanks," Cord called back with a chuckle.

"Don't mention it."

Honey wasn't paying attention. This was worse than seeing him in the full light of day. She was in his bed, a bed bathed in shadows, and she felt mesmerized by his body. The gentle rise and fall of his chest, the ripple of his muscles when the breath entered and left his body, held her gaze. The way the light and darkness moved over his skin enthralled her.

She was beginning to suspect he wore nothing under the sheet. The outline of his muscular legs was too clear, too defined. Lord, she was going crazy. All she wanted at that moment was to make a quick, dignified exit. No, that wasn't what she wanted at all.

Cord turned onto his back, his hands clasped behind his head, his eyes half closed. He was fascinated by the changing expressions on Honey's face, and he had a feeling she'd be embarrassed if she knew just how well he could see her. The sheet dipped lower as he moved, but he made no move to pull it up.

"Did you . . . have a nice trip?" Honey managed to choke out. She tried to look anywhere but at the virile body which kept drawing her eyes like a magnet. She couldn't help but watch the movements of his body when he answered her.

"It was tiring. We traveled around the Sound and down the coast, visited Phesner's, and I was able to get a better idea of what your situation is. So, how did you do at cleaning your office and finding your books?" He could see Honey wasn't even aware of how she was staring, but he was enjoying it, perhaps too much. Bending one knee, Cord rested his foot on the bed, concealing his response.

His question brought her out of her daydreams. Her distress showed clearly before she was able to mask it.

"I keep trying, Cord, but it doesn't seem to help much. I'm making headway though. I found the books, under 'M' in the filing cabinet. You know, 'M' for Money."

A chuckle escaped him, and once again her gaze was

captured and she found herself watching his chest ripple with his movements.

"It's okay, little Honey, we'll get it straight."

Women had looked at him before, some had aroused him, most hadn't, especially the blatant ones. But the way Honey was looking at him was different. She was seeing him as a man. Not a bank account or a savior for her show, but a man. That knowledge pleased, excited, and aroused him.

Unable to stop herself, Honey reached out to touch the dark, curling hair on his chest. She was so intent on discovering its texture that she didn't see how still Cord had become.

"It's so . . . soft . . ." Honey's voice trailed off. In embarrassment, she jerked her hand away and lowered her eyes.

Cord received the message she hadn't intended to send. He knew there had been no one since her husband. He was willing to bet there had been no one before, either.

A coiled tension released itself within his chest. He felt a wellspring of undefinable emotions rushing in, emotions he didn't want to analyze. So he settled on the one emotion he understood, the one he was ready to deal with. A gentle smile curved his lips. Reaching out, he picked up her braid and stroked the softness of her hair with his fingers. Then, he brushed her arm with the end of the braid.

"Honey, I want you."

"What . . . ?" She hadn't expected him to say such a thing, and she suddenly found she didn't know how to respond. Her mind settled on just one thought. Did he mean *right now*?

"Easy, Honey, I'm not going to jump you."

"But you said . . ."

"I just thought you should know. When we're together

we're combustible. I've had time to think about it, and I've come to the conclusion that I'd like to . . . well, you know." He dropped her braid and looked away. He hadn't expected to be uncomfortable or embarrassed, but she was looking at him with such wide, innocent eyes.

"Anyway, Honey," he continued. "I'm not looking for love and commitment. I had that once, and, well, . . ." Cord felt his voice catch, and cursed himself. He wasn't handling this right. He knew it. It sounded like he was trying to buy a used car. Lord, what a thought. Honey would probably punch him if she knew what he was thinking.

"What happened to make you so wary of love and commitment, Cord? Can you talk about it?" she managed to ask.

She chose to ignore the implied suggestion that they make love. Though her body might be willing, almost disgustingly willing, her mind wasn't. She knew she couldn't throw away everything she believed in for a brief fling, especially with a man who might be gone tomorrow.

And yet, she felt driven to understand what made Cord the way he was. She already knew parts of it. He'd been in love and his fiancée was killed in a crash. But what had made him run from his family, from himself? What kind of guilt, what demon, drove him?

Looking at Honey, or rather what he could see of her since the room had gotten darker and streetlamps no longer illuminated it, Cord felt an overwhelming desire to talk to someone, to talk to her. It was so much easier to talk in the dark.

"I told you my fiancée died last year," he stated as he sank further into the softness of his bed. He stared up in the direction of the ceiling, but his mind was seeing Gina.

"Yes," Honey replied, her voice softly encouraging, even though no answer was required. She sat up beside him on the bed, facing him, and crossed her legs Indian-style.

"Well, she died two months before we were supposed to be married. She was flying down from Maryland to meet me. I didn't feel I could get away from the aviation convention I was attending in Virginia Beach. Her plane went down in a storm, but it was a storm she never should have been flying in. It was my fault, all of it," he stated with certainty.

Honey heard the pain, the guilt, in his deep gravelly voice.

"Cord, there was nothing you could have done. No way you could have prevented what happened," Honey stated with certainty.

"But there was," he whispered on a tortured breath.

"How?" Honey questioned softly and with infinite gentleness.

"I could have loved my business less, could have married her sooner. We waited two years, *two years*, and it was all my fault."

"*What* was your fault? Did she want to marry you sooner?"

"Yes," he admitted. "I . . . she was going to school, getting her degree, and it was important to her. She lived on campus at the University of Maryland. She came home during the holidays to stay and visit her father, and we saw each other as often as we could. I thought it would be better to wait until she got her degree before we got married. I wanted to give her a chance to be sure, to let her realize her . . ."

"Her dream, Cord?"

"Yes. But we could have married sooner. It was a damned stupid decision. We really didn't have to wait. We would have been together, and . . ." His scratchy voice trailed off. He'd told Honey things he'd never told anyone else, not even Ronnie.

"And Gina would be alive?" Honey prompted, beginning to suspect what he'd tortured himself with all these months.

"Yes, dammit, she'd be alive. If I'd married her, she wouldn't have been on her way to see me in the middle of that damned storm. And if I hadn't worked so hard, I'd have been with her. Don't you understand? It was my fault!" he cried, springing to a sitting position, his hands clenching into fists that came to rest on his thighs. His breath came in quick, desperate pants, and sweat covered his body.

"All I see, Cord, is a man who's blamed himself for something he couldn't have stopped."

"You don't . . ." he began harshly.

"Cord," Honey broke in, her hand going out to cover one of his clenched fists. "At anytime in that two-year period, Gina could have insisted you marry her. Wouldn't you have done it?"

"Of course," he responded in bewilderment.

"You were trying to build a solid foundation for your future, and you worked hard all the time, didn't you?"

"Yes."

"And she knew it, didn't she?"

"Yes."

"Did you tell her you'd come home as soon as you could?"

"I . . . yes, I did," he replied as the memory of that phone call returned.

"And yet *she* chose to go out in that plane. She chose not to wait."

"Yes," he whispered in pain.

"Then, Cord, the guilt you've been feeling was for no reason," Honey concluded gently.

"But I killed her!"

"No, you didn't!" Honey cried fiercely, reaching out to take hold of his shoulders. She turned him to face her and gave him a shake.

"You didn't do a damn thing, Cordell Wayne. You loved a woman who had a dream, and you were man enough to give her a shot at that dream, to not be so selfish as to ask her to give it up. And she agreed, too. You weren't in on that decision alone. The night she died, if she had waited for you to return, the crash never would have happened. But, Cord, that doesn't mean she wouldn't have died."

"But . . ."

"Cord, when it's your time, it's your time. Whether you die in a car wreck, a plane crash, or just fall down the stairs and break your neck, nothing you do will save you when it's your time to go. Stop blaming yourself for something you had no control over. It wasn't your fault."

Cord was silent for so long, she began to wonder if he was even listening to her, if he had heard a word she said.

"I . . . you might be right," he finally said, his voice hesitant as he struggled with things he had spent the last year believing.

"Not *might*, Cord. I'm seeing this clearer than you are because you're too close. You've been forgetting one important fact. We all have choices to make, every day, and no one is responsible for the choice another person makes. You didn't cause her death. You didn't kill her. It was an accident, nothing more, nothing less."

"I . . . I guess it was." Why hadn't he seen it before? How had he managed to convince himself there was something he could have done to prevent Gina's death? It hadn't been his fault.

With a deep, shaky breath, Cord released the pent-up tension that remembering always caused. The guilt he had lived with for the past year began to fade. And as it faded, he began to heal, to let go of the past.

Cord became aware of Honey's hands on his shoulders. Instinctively, he reached for her and his hands spanned her waist. He settled her on his lap, curving his arms around her and holding her close.

"Thank you, Honey," he said, resting his cheek on top of her head.

"I didn't do anything," she murmured, snuggling her face against the softness of the hair on his chest.

"Oh, yes, you did, lady. You helped me realize things I hadn't even thought of."

"Did it help?"

"I'll let you know."

His husky voice sent a tingle down her spine. With heart-stopping tenderness, he placed his fingers under her chin and raised her face to his own.

NINE

Cord's lips met Honey's in a kiss of thanks, of suppressed emotion, and of restrained passion. When he moved away again, Honey sighed and quickly tucked her head under his chin.

The feel of her slender, slightly rough palm and fingers stroking his chest was a temptation he didn't need in his present state of mind. Ronnie was up front, driving the RV, heaven only knew where considering how long they'd been moving. Cord knew now was not the time to discover what he felt for Honey. He was too confused, his emotions too raw.

"Honey, you want to play doctor? I promise to be a very cooperative patient," he teased, trying to lighten the mood.

Honey laughed softly and regretfully moved out of his arms and off his lap. Her body's response to Cord never ceased to amaze her. However, this wasn't the time or the place.

"Sorry, but I'll have to decline," she replied as she slid off the bed and stood.

"Too bad. Well, if you'll wander up front, I'll get

dressed and find out what's taking Ronnie so long to get to your place.''

"Sure.''

"Honey,'' he called. When she paused in the doorway, he continued. "I still want you, you know. All this hasn't changed that.''

"Yes. I know.'' Her reply was soft, almost lost in the sound of the RV's engine, but not so soft that he didn't hear her.

Honey turned away without another word, shutting the sliding partition behind her. Thoughtfully, she negotiated the hallway, bumping into walls until she got the feel of the motor home's swaying motion. When she reached the couch, she allowed the vehicle's movement to dump her onto the well-worn cushions.

"He up?'' Ronnie questioned.

"Yes, of course, I was just talking to him,'' she replied absently. Hearing Ronnie's wicked chuckle brought her head up. "Just what do you think we were doing back there?'' she asked, ready to defend Cord if she had to.

"Weeeellll, that's why I was askin'.''

"Cool it, Ronnie,'' Cord said as he dropped onto the couch beside Honey. "And where the heck are you taking us? In the time you've been driving, we could have been to Honey's house at least five times.''

"Yeah, well, seemed like you guys was too busy to be bothered,'' Ronnie shot back.

Cord grunted a response that Ronnie didn't hear, then turned to Honey.

"What are you thinking about, Honey?'' The breathy whisper of his voice tickled her ear, startling her.

"Wha—?'' Honey's head jerked up, her lips grazing his when she twisted to face him. She pulled away from the contact and watched his eyes fire to life before he could conceal his expression behind friendly neutrality.

"Where was your mind, Honey?"

"Not far." She wasn't about to admit she had been thinking of him, of what he said. Honey frowned as she caught sight of the bruise on his jaw; even with the dim light from the kitchenette, it was easily discernible.

Leaning forward, she hesitantly touched the yellowish-purple mark marring the left side of his face. Unreasonable anger surged through her at the thought of someone hurting Cord.

"How'd you come by this bruise?" she questioned abruptly, her tone sharp.

"I had a little disagreement." Cord shrugged. A smile played about his lips at her fierce reaction.

The bruise itself didn't bother him, and it was healing well. He figured it wouldn't even be noticeable in a week or so. However, each time Ronnie saw it, he lowered his eyes, as though unable, or unwilling, to face the result of his rage.

"Don't worry, Honey. It doesn't hurt, and I'm fine."

His reassurance didn't help to ease her anger. She knew Cord could take care of himself, but the next time someone dared . . .

"Honey, forget it," he murmured softly, close to her ear.

With his voice so deep and sexy, how could she help but honor his request, especially now that her anger had been replaced with tingling shivers of arousal?

Softly, so Ronnie couldn't hear over the noise of the engine and his rock-music station, he continued. "I'd rather get back to our previous discussion. Are you mad at me?"

"No, Cord." Honey's reply was equally soft.

"Are you upset by what I said?"

"About what?"

"Wanting you."

"No, Cord."

"Do you want me, too?"

"N—" Biting her lower lip, Honey's liquid eyes met his probing stare.

"You don't have to answer," he said quickly.

"Yes, I think I do," she replied after a small hesitation. "We've shared a lot in the time you've been at the show, not the least of which is a physical attraction it would be stupid to deny. Do I want you? Yes. Will I take you? I don't know. You see, even before we talked tonight, I sensed something in you, a withdrawal, a tendency to change the subject, when things become too intense. I can't fight that. You have to deal with the part of you that would rather run away. But on my side, I know I'll never make love to someone I don't love. You want me now, Cord, but please don't take me unless you'll want me tomorrow as well. Okay?"

After a moment's hesitation, Cord nodded in agreement. "I can respect your feelings, Honey. For as long as I'm here, I promise not to push you farther than you want to go, but that's all I can promise. You're the first woman I've felt this way about in a long time, and if you came to me, I know all the good intentions in the world wouldn't keep me from taking you."

"Fair enough, Cord." Honey's smile was weak. "I understand."

He couldn't know that she wanted to go as far as he'd take her and principles be damned. But she knew it was better this way. He had no intention of staying, no matter what happened between them. Until he dealt with all the demons inside him, he wouldn't be ready to settle down anywhere. And did she really want him to stay? She felt things for him she didn't totally understand, but did she love him? She just didn't know.

"Hey, don't you guys know it's rude to whisper?" Ronnie grumbled.

"Shut up and drive," Cord snapped playfully.

"Why? We're here already."

"Smart aleck."

"Yeah, but what would you do without me?" Ronnie grinned.

"I'd like to find out sometime."

Honey's laughter filled the RV with sunshine, and Cord smiled, glad the worried frown had left her face.

"Come on, you two, I'll fix dinner. It's the least I can do to thank you for bringing me home."

"Great!" Ronnie exclaimed in enthusiastic agreement. He rocketed out of the RV before Cord could object.

But for once, Cord had no intention of objecting.

To the onlookers gazing skyward in rapt attention, the announcer's voice became nothing more than the persistent buzzing of a fly. Three skydivers hung suspended in midair, linked in a triplane, three-canopy stack. Their red-and-neon-blue air-foil parachutes were clustered together, and moved as one entity. A fourth jumper was spiraling earthward, trailing a stream of bright red smoke, but he wasn't as interesting as the death-defying cluster of sky divers.

Cord stood watching from farther away, removed from the spectators. His fists were clenched at his sides, his stomach tight, his breath quick and uneven. He knew there were skydivers who had died while performing a stunt like this. They'd become tangled, their parachutes had collapsed, and they'd fallen to their deaths. And now Honey was up there, involved in that dangerous stunt while the audience looked on, waiting for a disaster which would both horrify and thrill them.

He knew the people didn't want to see someone die.

They came to see people who took chances and survived. They came to be amazed and to cheer at each victory. But it was the fine line between success and disaster, especially at airshows, that captivated audiences. Only he wasn't captivated. He was paralyzed with fear. Honey was up there—thousands of feet off the ground. Her life hung at the end of a rectangular piece of air-inflated material. She was in danger, and there wasn't a damn thing he could do but stand by and helplessly watch.

When the skydivers separated and floated like feathers to land, one by one, on the large white "X" laid out on the fairgrounds, Cord finally drew a deep breath of relief. Had he known what Honey meant to attempt, he would have tied her up to keep her on the ground. But since arriving at the airshow, he'd spent so much time trying to bury himself in work, and avoid being alone with her, that he hadn't seen her practice sessions. Maybe if he had watched, had known, he could have stopped her from attempting the jump.

The announcer was drawing attention to the two hot-air balloons on either side of the field. Rainbow-striped, they swayed against the deep-blue sky. Young and old, fascinated by the sight, began to drift away from the center of the field to see the newest attraction at the fair.

In their wake, Cord stalked across the trampled grass, his only thought to get to Honey. He didn't question his unreasonable anger, or the fear which still gnawed at his gut. Last night, after another delicious dinner and companionable conversation, he and Ronnie had spent the night parked in her drive, and he'd refused to think about what had happened earlier. For the first time in a long time, he'd felt at peace. Well, he wasn't feeling very peaceful today.

Honey's long golden braid shone brightly in the sunlight as she pulled the red helmet from her head. Wives and friends rushed to take the collapsed parachutes from the skydivers and help them unfasten their leg and chest straps. Honey stepped out of her harness, bantering back and forth with Pete, Rudy, and Billy Joe. The crowd was dispersing around them, no longer awed by mere humans once again standing on solid ground. A few stopped to have their programs autographed or to congratulate them on the jump, but they moved away and soon only Honey's crew and friends were left.

"What the hell did you have to do *that* stunt for?" Cord snapped from behind her.

"What?" Honey spun around to find Cord barreling down on her. "Cord, how'd you like the jump?" Smiling triumphantly, Honey's laugh bubbled to the surface.

"You could have killed yourself!"

Honey's eyes widened in surprise, and she couldn't believe what she saw. He was furious. "Cord, what's wrong? We're all just fine."

"That's not the point," Cord rasped as he reached her and grabbed her by the shoulders. "Men have died doing that stunt! I couldn't believe it when you went into formation."

Giving in to an uncontrollable urge, he wrapped his arms around her, resting his chin on top of her head. He swallowed with difficulty, thanking heaven she was once again safe on the ground.

"You were scared." Honey's voice was soft, tinged with surprise.

"You're damned right I was. Why do *you* have to do the jumps?"

"As it is, Billy Joe and Rudy pull double duty. We just don't have enough jumpers, Cord."

"You will have."

"I can't aff—"

"*We* can afford them." It might not be the most sound

investment he'd ever taken on, but he'd decided to act on his instincts. He wanted to give her the help she needed. He wanted to find a way to keep her safe.

"*We*?" Honey questioned uncertainly.

"We."

"You're accepting my show? You want the partnership?" Honey cried in growing excitement.

"Yes."

Honey's arms went around his neck, pulling him down to plant a jubilant kiss on his mouth.

Cord's arms tightened around her, his lips lingering to kiss her once again, and then a third time.

"Hey, you two puttin' on a sideshow or just necking for the fun of it?"

"Ronnie, you've got lousy timing," Cord grumbled.

"No, I don't. I figured it was better to stop you before you forget where you're standin'."

"Thanks, Ronnie," Honey murmured with a sigh.

"No problem, half-pint. Let's go back to the RV. The balloons are off, Rudy and Billy Joe ain't scheduled to fly for a couple hours, and people are just going to be wanderin' around the rest of the fair. I'm hungry."

"Okay, okay," Cord and Honey caroled in unison. With their arms linked together, they followed Ronnie to the RV.

"I still haven't forgotten your office."

Honey blushed before she realized Cord hadn't been talking about *that*.

"That's our first order of business after we get everything stored away, repaired, and cleaned up after this show."

"Sure, Cord," Honey replied dutifully, hiding her reluctance. Warmed by his earlier concern, she would have accepted his decision to burn her office with little argument.

"There are a few things we need to discuss," Cord began as they reached the RV. "Let's sit out here."

He led her to one of the lawn chairs under the protective shade of the striped awning he and Ronnie had set up that morning. Ronnie had already disappeared into the motor home in search of food.

Honey sat down on the edge of one of the chairs. Some of her euphoria faded. She remembered, quite reluctantly, that having Cord agree to the partnership was not her main concern, at least not anymore.

Cord took the chair next to hers and turned it so they were facing each other. He took one of her hands between his calloused palms and looked into her eyes. Her hand started to burn and tingle. Almost absently, she noticed how his forest-green sports shirt brought out the green in his hazel eyes. Today, his eyes were deeper, more compelling. He was so handsome he made her ache.

"Honey, there are three conditions to this partnership," Cord stated.

She forced herself to concentrate on what he was saying, trying to forget how he was unconsciously running his thumb back and forth along her index finger.

"And those conditions are?" she finally asked after realizing he was waiting for some reaction from her.

"You need to take responsibility for the show's management or agree to hire a manager."

Honey nodded in acceptance. "I want to try managing the show before I think of hiring anyone else." Though she didn't like paperwork, she liked bringing in a stranger even less. Of course, if *Cord* were to offer . . .

"Second," he continued, stopping her wayward thought half formed. Honey lowered her head and tensed. She knew what was coming. When she tried to pull her hand away from his, he wouldn't let it go.

"I want you to promise not to do any more dangerous jumps or stunts."

"Oh." Honey's head came up and she just stared at him. She felt his hand gripping hers and saw the intensity of his gaze.

It took her a moment to regroup before she even started to consider what he'd asked. Almost immediately, she knew she couldn't give him the promise he wanted. There was no telling when she would be needed to fill in for someone. The jumps were part of her business, an important part.

"I'm sorry, Cord, but I can't do that," she began, her voice tinged with regret. Her other hand came up to rest on top of his. Gently she squeezed the back of his hand as she continued. "This show is mine. How can I promise not to be involved in such a vital part of it?" Her eyes implored him to understand.

Cord couldn't imagine her not being involved. And that was his problem. All he kept seeing was her having an accident, being hurt, maybe even killed. He had no idea why it mattered so much, but the thought of anything happening to Honey was enough to make him break out in a cold sweat. He was just getting over the sight of her skydiving stunt. Holding her hand, feeling her other hand on his, helped convince him everything was all right. He knew he had no right to make such a condition. He knew it wasn't fair to her, no matter how much he might want to protect her.

"I'm sorry, Honey. I just wanted . . . Never mind. I withdraw the second condition." He also withdrew his hands from hers.

"And the last one," she asked, feeling strangely bereft now that he was no longer touching her.

Cord sat back. His eyes met hers, and she tensed.

"Billy Joe."

"Cord . . ." Honey began, knowing she had to stay rational. The moment she had been dreading had arrived. She had to find a way to convince him to keep Billy Joe on, to give him a chance to straighten out. "I don't want to keep an employee who is disrupting, and even hurting, my show. However, I can't fire Billy Joe, not like this. One of the things I love about having my business is the ability to treat people like people—to be concerned for them.

"I've talked to him, Cord, and he promised to do better. He won't tell me what's wrong, but something outside of work is tearing him up. I know it. I want to give him the rest of this season. If he hasn't improved, I'll dismiss him. I have to give him a chance." Honey reached out and laid her hand over his where it rested on his thigh. She needed him to see her side, but not as much as she needed to touch him, to feel connected to him.

Cord was surprised she had spoken so calmly, never raising her voice or allowing her emotions to rule her on this issue. He was also proud and pleased.

After their first argument over Billy Joe, Cord knew he couldn't use threats. He couldn't carry them out, not with Honey. Today, he had hoped they could reach a compromise. Honey's solution was perfect. He smiled.

"Okay, Honey, if that's the way you want it."

"Are we still going to be partners?" she asked hesitantly, her compelling brown eyes never leaving him, her hand still covering his.

"Yes, of course," he replied as if there had never been any question.

Honey grasped his hand and brought it up to place a brief kiss on the back of it. She stood, still not releasing his hand, and smiled down into his bemused eyes.

"Ready for lunch? I'm starved."

Cord let her pull him up and docilely followed her into

the RV to join Ronnie. Somewhere, somehow, he knew he'd lost control. But for some reason, he just didn't care.

Honey felt her aching muscles relax. The shifting pillow of sand beneath her dark-blue beach blanket cushioned her tired body. She didn't know how Cord stood the pace. For the past week, each morning when she entered the hangar, he was already at work calling people, working out the specifics of their contract, interviewing new people for the show.

Just watching him could exhaust her. Well, not exactly. Watching Cord created an altogether different reaction. She pictured Cord in her mind, his dark-brown hair looking as though he'd run his fingers through it more than once, his hazel eyes alight with mischief. She could see the muscles of his chest flex and tense beneath the light-blue sports shirt he'd worn that morning. She could see the way his jeans hugged his behind and revealed his muscular thighs and more.

She felt her breasts peak against the material of her white bikini top and ignored the telling response. She felt the flowing warmth in her abdomen and a tingling along her skin, as though he was there beside her, watching her. But Cord was safely back at the hangar, working.

"Mind if I join you?"

Honey flipped onto her stomach so fast her white-rimmed sunglasses flew off. She knew that voice.

Squinting up against the bright sunlight, Honey fumbled for her sunglasses. Once she perched them on her nose, she started to look up. When she saw his bare, hairy legs, she gulped. Slowly she traced their well-muscled length with her eyes. Her gaze lifted and quickly skimmed over his green close-fitting swim shorts. When she got to his lean, washboard stomach and the width of his bare hair-covered chest, she could feel her heart beating like a conga drum against her rib cage. She gulped again when he leaned down closer to her.

"Can I join you," Cord repeated, suppressing the smile Honey's stunned expression demanded.

"Uh, sure."

Cord lay down on his back beside Honey. Propping himself up on his elbows, he watched the ocean for a few moments then took a deep stress-relieving breath.

"This was a good idea. I was looking for you, and Matt said you'd gone home. When I saw you out here, it looked like a perfect way to forget the world."

"I've always thought so," Honey replied, having gotten hold of herself once again. However, she remained on her stomach and simply closed her eyes and rested her cheek against the beach blanket.

"I hope you don't mind me intruding."

"No." How was she supposed to tell him she minded, a lot? Fantasizing about Cord was one thing, especially when he was miles away. Seeing Cord so unexpectedly, and in so little attire, sent intense arousing heat to every part of her body. It wasn't a welcome sensation, not with him so close, and not after all the lectures she'd given herself on control in the last week. Cord had kept his promise. He made no attempt to seduce her, even when they were alone in her beach house. In fact, he made no attempt to touch her at all!

Honey peeked over at Cord and bit the inside of her lip. Cord lay back, as relaxed as a sleek, well-fed jungle cat, and crossed his arms under his head. His arms were strong, well formed, not too muscular nor too thin. She wanted those arms around her. She wanted to curl up against his chest. Even the dark hair under his arms tempted her to touch it. It looked so soft, so silky. She closed her eyes quickly. The air carried his scent—clean, musky, with a hint of the spicy aftershave he wore. The silence seemed to sizzle with unspoken emotion.

"How are things going?" she asked to break the silence.

"Fine. Are you pleased with the progress we're making? Pretty soon you're going to have several new employees and the chance you wanted."

Honey smiled, thinking of the show. "Things are moving at a more hectic pace than I thought they would," she replied. "However, I'm not disappointed. You impress me as the kind of man who gets the job done, and who gets it done fast."

"Well, I guess that's a compliment, but I would have preferred one that was a bit more detailed. Oh, like maybe, 'Cord, you are just fantastic at managing business affairs, and I really admire your commanding presence and leadership, and the way you handle people.' " Cord's voice was raised in a ridiculous falsetto, and Honey laughed.

"Okay. Cord, you are just fantastic . . ."

Cord moved with lightning reflexes and had her pinned on her back in seconds. One of his legs was thrown over hers, and he half lay across her torso, his left hand braced on the blanket under her right arm. The rest of her teasing speech disappeared from her mind. She looked up into Cord's face and froze, mesmerized by the lighthearted smile curving his lips, the laugh lines that fanned out from his twinkling, teasing eyes.

"I think a heartfelt, 'You're wonderful, Cord' will do."

"You're wonderful, Cord," Honey replied dutifully, but meant it.

"That's better. I knew you'd see it my way," he said with a husky, satisfied chuckle.

Honey made a face, crinkling her nose and then frowning up at him from behind her sunglasses. She shoved at his shoulders to push him away, surprised and a little disappointed when he moved away without protest. She sighed.

"You're an idiot."

Cord gave her a reproachful look. "You're slipping again."

Honey shook her head and sat up, wrapping her arms around her bent knees. "What has you in such a good mood, you nut?"

"I don't think I'll tell you. That's two insults in less than a minute. I was better off when I had you pinned."

"Cord!" Honey grabbed a handful of sand and held it up threateningly.

"Okay. Okay."

Both of Cord's hands went up, palms out in surrender. His deep masculine chuckle filled the air and Honey dropped the sand.

"Now, what's happened?" she asked, having been infected with his good humor.

"Well, I found someone crazy enough to do a wing-walking routine."

"Really? Oh, Cord, that's wonderful. Did you hire them? When do they start? What's their name?"

"Whoa, slow down." Cord sat up to face Honey, who was now kneeling beside him, almost bouncing up and down in excitement.

"His name is Larry Kingston, and that wasn't all my news, you know."

"What news could be better?" Honey asked, wide-eyed with anticipation.

"Well, he's quitting Phesner's to work for the Johnson Airshow."

"Great! That's got to be the best news I've had in months, other than you taking the partnership, of course. And it serves Phesner right, too, that slimy little slug."

Cord's brows came together in question and his indulgent smile disappeared. "Slimy? What did he do?"

Honey hesitated, just realizing what she'd said. She ducked her head to hide her blush.

"Honey? Tell me what happened."

"Nothing really," she began, reluctant to talk about it. "A year ago, he showed up at the hangar. He caught me as I was locking up and asked why I kept trying to make my 'rinky-dink' show work. He offered to merge with me and take care of me."

Something in her voice, in the offhand manner of her explanation, didn't sit well with Cord. His brows came together again, this time in a frown.

"And was he talking about just the show in that 'merger'?" Cord questioned, his voice clipped.

Honey didn't raise her head. She started playing with the blanket, moving the sand around under it.

"Honey?"

"I, well, I thought so at first. I told him no. Then, he put one of his greasy hands on my shoulder and leered at me with his little pig eyes. When I tried to move away, he wouldn't let me," she finally admitted, a trace of remembered fear in her voice, even after all this time.

"Did that slimy little bastard hurt you?" Cord demanded.

TEN

The question, and Cord's tone, brought her head up. She met his angry gaze and her lips parted in surprise.

"No, Cord, he didn't hurt me." She was amazed when he seemed to relax after her answer. The blazing anger left his eyes.

"What happened when he wouldn't let you go?" he questioned, his voice calmer.

"Matt came back. He had forgotten his toolbox, and he needed it to work on his wife's car. Charlie Phésner left real fast when Matt stepped up to ask why he had his hand on me. Matt is about six inches taller and forty pounds heavier than Phesner."

"Though I saw his show, I never met the . . . man. Has he come back?"

Once more, Honey didn't answer. She looked out toward the waves.

"He came back," Cord stated, his voice low, dangerous. "What did he do?" His voice rose, each word distinct. Seeing her tense, he took a deep breath. "Tell me," he said more gently.

"He just . . . Cord, can we talk about something else?"

149

"Yes, as soon as you tell me what he did."

Honey shook her head at his persistence and bit her lower lip.

"He made another offer. I said no again. Then he threatened to steal my bookings and to see that no one worked for me. He also made some insulting comments. Billy Joe overheard him and threw him up against the wall. Phesner threatened to have Billy Joe arrested, but you've seen how Billy Joe can be. He was ready to 'smear Phesner all over the hangar,' and he said as much." Honey smiled at the memory of Phesner's little eyes bulging half out of their sockets in fear.

"After hearing that, I don't feel so bad about keeping Billy Joe on. I'll have to thank him the next time I see him. Did Phesner come back after that?"

"No."

"Good. When was that last time, Honey?"

"Two months before I applied to Wayne and Cray for help."

Cord said nothing, just stared at her for a moment.

"I was your last hope, wasn't I?"

Honey met his gaze and didn't even attempt to lie. "Yes," she said simply. "The banks wouldn't touch us. Phesner made good on his threats. We've lost some of our bookings because of him, and when I advertise for help, he advertises, too, and tops my offers."

"Forget about Phesner. I'll handle him." Cord's eyes narrowed, and a dangerous half-smile curved his lips.

"What are you . . ."

"Don't worry. Now, back to my good news." Cord changed the subject, acting as though the previous conversation never occurred. Even his expression changed, and his eyes twinkled with good humor. "Your books are finally up to date, assuming, of course, that you don't have two years of lost bills under all the junk in your office."

Honey was left no time to puzzle over Cord's strange behavior. She flushed but brought her chin up in response. "I might be a lousy manager in your opinion, but I did keep the stack of bills and receipts together. I had to, the I.R.S. wouldn't accept 'cluttered office, unable to find' as a valid excuse."

"Fair enough. According to the accountant, you're only a little in the red. However, with the expenses this season, you were right in assuming you wouldn't have a business next year. With your current bookings, and my investment, you'll be fine."

"Next year will be the test. I know that." Honey was nervous enough about that fact. "We've got to start contracting for next year's shows, and Phesner has already stolen my most profitable booking for July fourth of next year."

"I've been making calls, outlining the new format we talked about. I've got some possibles already lined up. After you do your show at the Wayne and Cray Airfield, your phone should ring off the hook. I figure you'll be turning down offers all along the East Coast."

Honey looked up and caught the boyish enthusiasm on Cord's face and smiled in gratitude. She didn't know what she'd have done without him. "Thank you, Cord. It's like a dream."

"Honey, you'll work damn hard for this dream, I guarantee it. Don't thank me. You don't have any reason to." And the last thing he wanted was her gratitude.

"Was that the last of the good news?" She was almost afraid to ask. She didn't know if she could stand any more.

"Yep, except the contracts are ready to sign. Your lawyer and mine will be at the hangar tomorrow at ten sharp. Any problems with the contract?"

"No. It's pretty standard. You get a forty-nine percent

interest in the show. You give me the capital and assistance I need in exchange for a share in the profits and a say in all major decisions. When I'm able, I can buy you out, or I can keep the partnership. I liked that clause. I think the contract is more than fair.''

"Good. Now that we've handled business, and wasted a lot of this beautiful sunshine, what do you say we forget the airshow and just take a swim?''

"Yes to forgetting, no to the swim."

"Why?"

"I, uh, can't swim," she admitted, almost embarrassed to do so when she lived on the beach. But she didn't want Cord to think she didn't want to be with him, not when the opposite was true.

"You can't . . . but you love the ocean."

"Yes. I like flying, too, but you don't see me trying it without a plane."

"Didn't you ever learn to swim?" he asked, almost as if he were asking if she knew how to walk.

"I can paddle around a little and stay afloat, but I'm not strong enough to swim alone. If I got caught in a riptide . . .'' She shuddered at the thought.

Cord didn't much care for the mental image, either. He frowned. "Come on then and paddle. I'm an excellent swimmer," he said, then stood and waited for her, his hand outstretched to help her up.

Honey gave him her hand automatically and when she was standing beside him, she took off her sunglasses and dropped them into her straw beach bag.

"Uh, Cord, I don't think I should. I usually just sunbathe. I've never even gotten this suit wet."

"Then it's high time you did." It was all the warning she had. He scooped her up and headed for the water. Cord looked down at the rather prim white two-piece—at least prim by today's standards. It covered her better than a bra and panties would have. On Honey, it was the sexiest swimsuit he'd ever seen.

Honey was too surprised to protest. Then she simply resigned herself. The wicked smile she caught curving Cord's lips told her he expected her to struggle. Instead, she chose to enjoy the feel of his arms around her, his chest hair tickling her side. She wrapped her arms around his neck.

He was so strong, so beautifully masculine. She could see the muscles in his arms bulging. She wanted to touch them, to trace their contours. But she knew if she did, their time together would turn into something she wasn't sure she was ready for. Cord had been specific on that point. If she started something, she had to be sure. She wasn't.

Honey felt the cool bite of the water swell over her stomach. It shocked her and made her tighten her hold around Cord's neck. Her body was practically covered with water, and each wave rocked her against Cord's chest. The refreshing coolness was a welcome relief after baking in the sun, and when Cord made no move to drop her, she relaxed, secure in his arms. Cord would protect her.

"You should be able to stand here," Cord murmured gruffly.

He released his hold on her legs and Honey's lower body slowly sank until her feet touched bottom. She stood; the water covered her breasts and came up to Cord's chest. Honey's hands were still resting on Cord's shoulders, his arm lay loosely around her back, his hand tucked under her arm, his fingers oh-so-close to her breast. A large wave swell pushed her body flush against Cord's. For a moment, they touched full length, thigh to thigh, breast to chest. She felt the bold pronouncement of his arousal, and her gaze met his. His eyes hid whatever he was feeling, and she quickly lowered her head, dropped her hands, and moved away. He let her go without saying a word, and she almost sighed in disappointment.

Honey moved closer to shore before she turned around. She found Cord swimming parallel to the shoreline, his strokes sure and powerful.

She began to dog-paddle halfheartedly. Now that Cord wasn't beside her, her enjoyment of the water had dimmed. She curled her legs under and then straightened them out in front of her, lifting her body into a back float. Her braid twirled and flowed around her as each wave lifted her, sent her toward shore, then brought her back out to sea again. She felt safe with Cord nearby. She only wished he was closer.

She knew it was crazy to want to keep Cord by her side, but she enjoyed his company. She liked being with him. Things were different when he was near, more exciting, more vibrant.

They had spent each night of the past week at her beach house, talking about the day's activities, laughing together, even arguing as they planned the show's future format. It had been fun. He had been wonderful. His judgment and his keen business sense never failed to amaze her. She learned so much just watching him deal with the day-to-day business of expanding and modifying her show.

Yet each night, after they finished dinner and Ronnie returned to the RV, she expected—something. Cord never touched her. When he'd taken her hand, had carried her into the water, she'd realized how much she had missed his touch this last week. It was strange how she'd grown accustomed to it so quickly.

It wasn't as if she hadn't enjoyed their nights together. She did. They never ran out of things to talk about. Once they exhausted the subject of work, they easily moved on to something else. She found him easy to talk to, and she enjoyed listening to his opinions and views, to stories from his travels. And yet, she wanted something more . . . More what?

Sighing, knowing she had no answers to the vague dissatisfaction plaguing her, Honey lowered her body and reached for the sandy bottom with her toes. It wasn't there.

In surprise, Honey went under and came up sputtering. Dog-paddling for all she was worth, she looked around and saw the beach, and the little spot where her blanket was laid out. It looked so tiny. How had she gotten so far out? She'd always been careful when she went into the water alone. What was she going to do?

A whimper of panic escaped her throat.

"Easy, Honey," came Cord's voice from close beside her.

She felt his hand rub her lower back and the panic faded. Cord was there. He wouldn't let anything happen to her.

"I want you to paddle slower. You're going to exhaust yourself if you don't."

Honey tried. She was surprised when her head stayed above water.

"How . . . how did you . . . ?"

"I saw you drifting out. I called to you, but you didn't hear me, so I followed you. You were a million miles away."

"Not that . . . far. The beach is, though."

"Nah. Let's head for it. I'll be right beside you all the way."

It seemed far away to her. She wasn't sure they'd make it. Well, Cord would. Why hadn't she paid attention? She would have never gone out so deep if she'd been in her right mind. But Cord had been with her. She'd been thinking of him.

She wasn't going to make it. Already she was exhausted.

"Honey, you know you can't keep avoiding that office of yours. It's a disgrace. In the next week, we're going to finish up the inventory and repairs. Then I expect you to buckle down. The only one who can do it is you. Who else knows where all the papers came from, or where they should go?"

"You could . . . help, you know."

"Not me, lady. My . . . momma didn't raise . . . no fool. That office is yours."

"I . . ."

Honey felt her strength flagging. She wasn't moving forward anymore, and the beach still looked so far off. Even Cord seemed tired. Then she remembered the rigorous swimming he'd done before she lost track of him. Suddenly, she didn't care about herself anymore. Was Cord okay?

"Honey," he said from beside her, and her name seemed so soothing when he said it. "I want you to turn over and float, okay? I'm going . . . to pull you along with me."

"Cord, I can't . . . I . . ." Looking up, she saw the suddenly fierce expression on his face.

"You just turn . . . over, and float. Don't argue," he commanded, his voice harsh.

Honey did as ordered. She felt his arm come around her, felt her body start to glide along on the water as his powerful muscles pulled them closer and closer to shore. She didn't know if moments or minutes had passed when Cord stopped. She wanted to reach out to him, to tell him it was okay.

She wanted to hold him, to thank him. She felt his hands on her waist, felt him pulling her closer. She lowered her feet but still couldn't feel bottom.

Cord pulled her close to his side and wrapped his arm

around her waist. She realized he was standing. He was panting with his own exertion, but he was on solid ground. He slogged through the water, and when she felt the bottom under her feet, she said a little prayer of thanks.

They stumbled toward her blanket, both collapsing onto it. Honey was trembling, more with reaction than fear.

"You are going to take swimming lessons, and water safety, and anything else the Red Cross or the YWCA offers," Cord ordered once he caught his breath.

"Yes, Cord," she replied without argument, her voice shaky.

"And if you go in the water again without me, I swear I'll beat you."

"Yes, Cord."

Cord raised his head and came up on his elbows to look over at her. She lay nearby, on her back, her eyes closed. But he could see the wet trail from her tears. She was trembling, and he felt the need to reassure her. He didn't want to think of how close she'd come to disaster. It hurt too much to think of it. He reached for her and pulled her against him, wrapping his arms around her. He needed to hold her, to know she was safe.

"Easy, baby. It's okay now," he said, his voice husky and intimate. "You scared the devil out of me when I saw you that far out."

"I scared the devil out of myself," Honey returned.

Cord smiled when he heard a trace of her usual spirit.

"I'm serious about those classes."

"I know. I'll take them." Honey couldn't voice how scared she'd been. She had almost killed them both with her lack of skill. The thought of losing Cord sent sharp pain knifing through her.

Honey pushed back to look at Cord. He kept his arms around her, and she felt warm, secure—alive.

"Thank you, Cord."

Their lips met, and Honey couldn't say who moved first. It was a kiss filled with things said and unsaid. She could feel the passion there, but it was restrained, tightly leashed. This was a reassurance of life, of the knowledge they were there, together. She never wanted to stop kissing him.

Cord reluctantly pulled away. He wanted nothing more than to lay back and strip that sexy swimsuit off her. To make love to her, here on the beach. But he'd made a promise. He glanced down at Honey and quickly looked away, to the waterproof watch he still wore.

"Honey, if you don't want to be embarrassed, you should probably go up and change now. Matt will be dropping Ronnie off soon. It's getting close to dinnertime."

Honey's eyes opened and it took a moment for his words to sink in.

"Embarrassed?" What did she have to be embarrassed about?

"That white swimsuit of yours is transparent when wet. It should have come with a warning label."

Honey pulled away and sat up, not believing him. She looked down and found he was right. Her gaze flew up to find Cord unashamedly enjoying the view, a wicked smile once more curving his lips.

With a gasp, she grabbed her towel out of her beach bag and wrapped it around her body.

"Men are pond scum," she stated as she stood and glared down at Cord.

Cord smiled innocently. "Nope, they're just excellent at designing swimwear."

Honey turned and marched away, not even dignifying that comment with a response. She was fighting hard not to laugh as she left Cord to gather up her beach things. Her muscles felt like jelly, but the fear was gone. In its place, a warm glow was growing. Cord.

*   *   *

"Honey? Honey, where are you?" Cord called from somewhere in the hangar.

Honey smiled, tilting back in her chair. The mountain of papers, books, correspondence, and *junk* effectively hid her petite form. In just two short weeks, she'd gone from hanging on to up and coming. The contracts were signed, and she'd acquired her partner.

The hangar was still a hive of activity. Her men had received an increase in pay and were busy finishing the inventory and the repairs. Three new people had been hired, specialists all three: one skydiver/pilot, one hang glider, and one balloonist (with her own balloon). They were all in addition to the wing walker/mechanic Cord had hired last week. Cord had recruited every one of them, and they'd all been hired from Phesner's.

The shows scheduled for this year were delighted to get the extra attractions, for no extra charge. Cord said it was a great advertising gimmick, and he was right. As he had predicted, some of his contacts had come through. The calendar was filling up for next year.

As for Cord, he'd become her partner, but also a very special friend as well. In the past two weeks, she'd discovered that they had similar tastes in music, food, and, of course, a mutual love of anything to do with flying. In fact, with the exception of baseball, which she'd always found to be totally boring, they agreed on just about everything.

But she wasn't stupid!

There was no way she was going to let Cord find her, especially today, not with what he was planning. It had been a stroke of luck, and a bit of Ronnie's help last week, that had enabled her to find all the papers necessary for the accountant Cord hired to update her books. Her office had suffered as a result.

Cord had started dropping hints last week, and she'd managed to ignore them. There had been more important things to worry about. Now, however, she knew Cord was stalking her. He was ready to chain her to a stake in the center of her office with only enough links in the chain to allow her to reach all four corners with a broom. There was no way she was going to let Cord find her just so she could start cleaning out her—no, *their* office. Especially not when he was partly to blame and he had no intention of helping.

As she thought of Cord, a gentle smile curved the fullness of her lips. He could be so sweet and understanding, so good and kind, so passionate and gentle. He was intelligent, perceptive, and generous. He was also a good man to have around if you needed help. The past two weeks with him had been wonderful, each day filled with promise, and each night with unfulfilled desire. Cord was so sexy, so appealing, and so honorable. She could not fault him there.

She was appalled to realize his noble intentions made her want to scream and smack him. She also wanted to hug him and tell him how special he was.

Since that night in his motor home, he had been relaxed, more at ease. He even seemed at peace, if that was possible. He joked more easily, seemed happier around the airfield, and he even seemed to enjoy, and seek out, her company. She knew somehow that he'd come to terms with Gina's death. He no longer avoided references to his business, or his old life at the Wayne and Cray Airfield. It made her feel warm and bubbly inside to think that even in a small way, she was the cause of the change in Cord. Now that he was no longer as reserved as before, now that he had opened up, he was intensely lovable . . . Lovable?

Honey froze, losing her balance and pitching forward, striking the mountain of papers with her outstretched hands. Piles of papers and magazines clamored to the floor around her. She didn't even notice. Stunned disbelief swept across her face.

"How did that happen?" her mind demanded. "Easily," her heart responded.

Slowly, a vibrant, pulsating awareness swept over her, shining from deep within her being. Suddenly it all made sense. All her unnamed longings and the vague disquiet and discontent she felt when Cord treated her as she thought she wanted to be treated, made sense; she wanted to be in his arms. She loved him! She loved Cord!

Cord entered the office and stopped short. The sound of the toppling avalanche from within had told him where to find her, in the last place he would have looked. Thanks to the papers and other junk that had crashed to the floor, he had a clear view of Honey, and she wasn't even aware he stood watching. Instead, she was wrapped in her own thoughts, and whatever they were, her joy glowed outward for all to see. With her mind elsewhere, she didn't notice his presence.

His gaze caressed her. She was so damn beautiful, almost too beautiful to be real.

Cord felt a tightening in his abdomen, felt his heart beating rapidly in his chest. The past two weeks had been hectic, the nights at Honey's beach house his only respite. He enjoyed the time he spent with her, and each time he found himself alone with her, he struggled to keep his promise. That afternoon on the beach had almost been his undoing. But the painful awareness he had struggled with for the past two weeks was mild compared to what he now felt. Never had he wanted her more. She seemed so vibrantly sensual, so unaware of her power, and he wanted her . . . now. But she had given him a new start, given him peace, and he had given her a promise. It was a promise he intended to keep.

Honey looked up, and the smile that touched her lips practically stopped Cord's heart.

"Hi, Cord," Honey murmured.

Cord shut the door behind him, not stopping until he stood beside her. "Were you hiding from me?" His voice came from deep in his chest, a sandy-soft rasp of unacknowledged emotion.

"Yes," Honey breathed, standing to face him, her head tilted back, her lips parted. Her tongue swept out to wet the dryness of her lips, wanting his kiss, needing it. She wanted to be held by the man she loved, to feel the security of being in his arms. She needed his touch . . . now.

Cord's eyes closed as he tried to stifle the raging need within him. He knew she wasn't aware of the innocent provocation of her movements. When he opened his eyes, he was under control.

"Since I've realized you won't clean this mess unless coerced, I'm going to help. We can begin now and finish tomorrow. I've been letting you slide, but it's time for you to get organized," Cord stated briskly, refusing to look at her again.

Honey huffed and blew a tendril of hair from her forehead. Looking around, she spied what she was searching for. With a devilish gleam sparkling in her eyes, she grabbed Cord's arm, tugging him along with her.

"Honey, wha—?"

"I need some help, Cord. You do want to help, right?" she questioned innocently.

"Sure, but . . ."

"Now, Cord . . ." she drawled. Reaching the stack of large books, she stepped up, turned gingerly, and flung her arms around Cord's neck, snuggling her head against his shoulder. She just held him, wanting to savor these first minutes with the newfound knowledge of her love for him.

Cord pushed her gently away, holding her shoulders. He looked eye to eye with her, watching in fascination while the endless depths of her doe-soft eyes darkened and fired with need. An answering need jumped within him, making him forget the questions he wanted to ask, the cleaning they had to do, everything but Honey. He pulled her closer, wrapping his arms around her. With Honey's breasts pressed against his chest, the hardening peaks burrowing into his thin shirt, rubbing his sensitive skin, he could think of nothing beyond his need and her apparent willingness. A groan escaped his throat.

Cord conquered her mouth with gentle savagery, plundering the rich treasures within. Feeling her lips parting, her hands delving into his hair, her body pushing more intimately against him, he shuddered with the force of his instant and painful arousal. He tried to withdraw before she denied him again.

Honey tightened her arms around him, refusing to let him go. When his tongue withdrew from its pursuit of her own, hers followed, exploring the intoxicating nectar in the warm cavern of his mouth. She wanted Cord, wanted to express her love for him, to give all that she could give to him, to give herself and all that she was. Her body ached for his, her soul called to his, and her heart and mind sought to merge with his own. Never had she wanted something so fiercely. Never had every particle of her being yearned to be joined to another the way it did with Cord. Nothing mattered but their love, and she knew he must love her. There was no other explanation for his caring, his tenderness, his restraint.

"Make love to me, Cord. Here. Now," she pleaded, her lips tracing the sensitive lobe of his ear.

"Yes, Honey . . . now . . ." Cord's voice was raspy, his words almost incoherent.

He pulled her slight weight against him, then set her on

her feet again, breaking their kiss. He locked the door at her gentle urging before losing himself in the passionate web being spun between them. His glazed eyes focused on her, seeing the sweetly curved fullness of her lips waiting for him, the slumberous brown of her eyes fired with golden sparks of need and longing, and something undefinable, something more . . .

His hands trembled as he reached for the front zipper of her coveralls. Slowly, the zipper rasped downward, parting the material, revealing the pure ivory and honey tones of her skin. Unable to resist the lushness hinted at by the exposed valley between her breasts, he stopped the zip at her waist and brushed the material from her shoulders.

Desire, hot and hungry, burned in his eyes. His throat tightened, catching his breath, refusing to let it escape. But as much as his body cried out for release, he couldn't bring himself to rush. He wanted to savor every intimate moment and every gloriously fulfilling discovery. Releasing his trapped breath in a deep sigh of satisfaction, Cord leaned forward to barely touch his lips to hers.

Honey watched Cord silently caress each part of her body with his eyes. She felt no shame, no embarrassment. The lacy peach bra she wore couldn't hide the effect his look had on her, but she felt no urge to shield her arousal from him. She wanted to be with him, to be one with him. When he touched her lips so tenderly with his own, she slipped her hands from the sleeves of her coverall, letting it slide over her hips to the floor. She pushed off her shoes and socks before reaching out to hold his face between her fingertips.

Cord's gaze flickered down her body, and he groaned and leaned his forehead against hers, closing his eyes as he fought for control.

"I . . . I want to go slowly, Honey. I want to savor

every moment before, after, and during the time I lose myself within your sweet body, but I don't know if I can . . ."

"It doesn't matter," Honey breathed, a smile of understanding curving her lips.

"But it does!" Cord cried in response, suddenly realizing just how true it was. "It matters, Honey . . . It matters."

Cord took her lips, unable to curb the strength of his passion for her mouth. He reveled in her answering need as she met and matched his urgent embrace. Impatiently, he reached for the hooks of her bra, wanting to feel her breasts against him, wanting to taste her as he had once before—so long ago, it seemed.

With a murmur of protest, Honey held his wrists, leading his hands to his sides. At his frown, her lips pursed in amusement. Grasping the hem of his light-blue cotton shirt, she lifted, easing his arms higher until she could pull the shirt over his head.

"I want to see you, Cord, feel you against me."

"Yes. Oh, yes!" Cord reached for her again, and the lacy bra fell to the floor at their feet, followed by her brief panties. He needed to feel her pliant and soft against him. But when he paused to explore the newly revealed treasures, his heart almost stopped at the sight of her voluptuous, sinfully sexy form.

"No woman should be so lovely," he breathed, unknowingly easing the brief trepidation she had experienced as she wondered if she would please him.

"Forgive me, darling Honey, I know I can't . . . I'm sorry . . ."

Seeing his fear of hurting her, the regret on his handsome face, made her ache. With a feminine growl, her small fingers curled into the thick darkness of his hair, pulling his head down. She arched against his body, her lips devouring his own in heated passion. Her hands slid down to the broad strength of his shoulders, her head lowered, following the path her hands took, giving in to her need to taste and touch every part of him. She wasn't worried he might hurt her; part of her knew he couldn't. Hopefully, she'd find a way to reassure *him*.

Pulling Cord closer, she explored the shape and texture of his back, his hair-roughened chest. She touched him as she'd wanted to that day on the beach, and still it wasn't enough. She slid against him, needing, wanting, loving.

"Cord!" she pleaded.

Cord unclenched his fists, releasing his control and allowing his need to govern. He grasped the soft, rounded firmness of her bottom, lifting her off the floor and settling her intimately against him. He captured her mouth with his, and in two strides, they were at the desk. Gently, he sat her on top of it, with its cushion of papers, never breaking their kiss.

While his fingers fumbled with the snap and zipper of his jeans, his lips nibbled at her own. Pushing the rest of his clothes from his body, he kicked his moccasins from his bare feet and stepped closer, parting her knees. His hands reached to cover her breasts, kneading their softness, and his lips left hers to trace a path down the sensitive skin of her neck, pausing to tease her there when she cried out and trembled against him.

Wanting to plunge into her softness, to sheath himself in her warmth and take away the aching emptiness of his body and soul, he couldn't, not without knowing if she was ready for him.

He bent his head to her breast, enveloping one turgid nipple into the warmth of his mouth. While he suckled gently, one hand slipped down her abdomen, teasing her thighs further apart.

Honey clutched Cord's shoulders as a helpless gasp escaped her throat. Her breath rasped in and out of her lungs when he discovered the yearning moisture at her center. His mouth left one breast only to torment the other, and his hands grasped her hips, pulling her closer. Papers slid to the increasing pile on the floor, but she never noticed. His mouth sought hers, his tongue plunging between her lips, his body arching forward, burying himself in her moist, velvet softness.

A purr of mutual satisfaction escaped their throats, but it wasn't enough for him. "Honey . . ."

"I know," she whispered, knowing it could be no other way for him, and not caring. She wanted this, too.

"You're so . . . soft . . . so warm and . . . tight . . ." Cord groaned, moving deep and hard and fast within her. Tucking his face against the scented hollow of her neck, he nipped and kissed the tingling area beneath her ear, his hands frantically pulling her closer, reaching, searching for more, and more . . .

Then, he found it. A surging wash of fulfillment exploded within him, leaving him drained and spent.

Slowly, awareness returned. Cord breathed deeply, his body still shaking with the intensity of his release. He became aware of Honey's arms wrapped around him, of the gentle kisses she was placing on his shoulder, and he groaned silently.

It had happened too soon. Though she'd been with him all the way, he hadn't fulfilled her, hadn't pleasured her. He'd lost control.

His arms wrapped around her slender back, and he buried his head against her shoulder, his body still joined with hers. He didn't want to leave her, not yet, not like this.

Honey felt a strange moisture on her skin. Reaching up to smooth Cord's hair, she couldn't believe what was happening. He couldn't be crying, not Cord.

"Cord? Are you okay?" she whispered.

"I'm sorry, Honey," Cord choked, not believing he could have been so selfish. "I wanted so much more for you. I wanted to please you."

"Cord, it's all right, really it is." Her own eyes misted with tears at his obvious concern for her, and her heart swelled with love.

"Cord? Cord, look at me," Honey urged, patiently prying his face from her shoulder and holding it between her palms. "You did please me. Very much." Seeing his sadness was too much for her. With a soft cry she pulled him closer, her lips and tongue tenderly removed the salty wetness from his cheeks.

When she looked up again, she found a strange light in the deep, swirling hazel of his eyes. She smiled, brushing at her own tears with the back of her hand. "Personally, I don't think we should clean this office; see how convenient a nice cushy desk can be?"

Cord saw the complete disarray of papers and files scattered around his feet and smiled. A chuckle escaped him.

"You're not getting out of it that easily, Honey," he warned.

Leaning forward, his lips brushed hers. "Thank you," he murmured.

Trailing his lips down her neck, Cord felt her shudder. Looking up, he smiled. "You're neck's very sensitive."

"Yes," she breathed.

"Uhmmm." He returned to his tantalizing exploration of that erogenous area. He continued to hold her on the desk with his hips still locked to hers, and his hands reached to explore the gentle slope of her back. Leaving her neck, he nuzzled her shoulder, tracing a path with the satiny rasp of his tongue.

"Cord!" Honey's womb contracted in reaction, and she

felt him within her, felt the change in him. She froze in shock.

Feeling her unnatural rigidity, he looked up in question. "What's wrong?" Worry darkened his eyes.

"Your . . . I mean you're still . . . I . . ."

"I know."

"But . . ."

"Last time was mine, this time's for you." A devilish fire flared in his eyes before he went back to his exploration of her trembling body.

"Oh, Cord," she sighed, wrapping her arms around his shoulders. Her legs tightened around him, locking around his hips. Once again, she lost herself in the hypnotizing, sensual magic of his touch.

ELEVEN

"Are you okay?"

"Mmm. More than okay," Honey replied dreamily, resting her head on Cord's shoulder.

They were sitting on her desk chair, where faded cloth cushions protected Cord's bare bottom and back from the vinyl, and Honey was nestled on his lap, content, unable to think of any place she'd rather be.

"I didn't mean for this to happen."

"What?" She raised guarded eyes to his face, trying to hide her sudden worry.

"Not this way," he reassured her.

"Oh."

"I mean on a desk. Here." Cord shook his head in self-disgust. He couldn't believe his lack of control. Thank heavens there weren't any windows in her office!

"I can't think of anywhere I'd rather be."

"How about a bed?" Cord suggested dryly, amused by her languid complacency.

"Uhmmm. That would be nice, but this, this was glorious." Honey fairly glowed with the memory of how Cord had made her delirious with pleasure, as if to atone for

171

the first time. Flushed with memories, she hid her face against his neck.

Cord chuckled, a self-satisfied smile curving his lips.

"I suppose now you're going to be insufferably arrogant," Honey grumbled as she caught sight of his smile. In truth, she didn't really care.

"Probably, but you won't mind once I show you we can do horizontally what we just did vertically."

"Oh!" Burying her face against his neck again, Honey couldn't suppress a shiver of excitement.

Cord fondly stroked the top of her head, a frown creasing his brow as he felt the braid. He would have loved to see her hair falling free around her shoulders and down her back while they made love.

Honey was content. Cord was everything she could have asked for, and hadn't even realized she needed. Before he came, the airshow had been her life. Now, even though she still loved the show, she loved Cord more. He made her feel complete.

"Cord, thank you for coming to the show. If it hadn't been for you, I never would have realized what was missing from my life." She sighed and snuggled more closely into the curve of Cord's warm body.

"Sex?" Cord asked with a teasing chuckle.

"No, you fool. Love. I love you so much, Cord," she murmured, placing a kiss on his neck.

Cord felt his body tense. She couldn't love him. She just couldn't. And he most definitely didn't love her. Just because he liked being around her, and his body responded to her as it had to no other woman, didn't mean he loved her. Did it?

She might have helped him realize that he'd been needlessly blaming himself for Gina's death, and he might have been grateful to her, but gratitude wasn't love. And the way she made him feel wasn't love. It just wasn't!

With an abrupt, jerky move, he rose from the chair, dumping Honey onto her feet without a word. He didn't look at her as he retrieved his clothes from the floor and started dressing.

Honey stared at Cord's back wordlessly. A dreadful premonition gripped her stomach, tying it into knots of apprehension. Suddenly embarrassed, she began gathering her clothes and dressing as well. When she finished, he still hadn't turned around. He just stood looking at the closed door, his back stiff and straight.

"Cord . . . ?" she began hesitantly. What had she done? She'd just been honest with him. She loved him. Was that so terrible?

"I . . ." he began, only to pause when his voice caught.

Slowly he turned to face her, and the closed, wary expression was back on his face. It made her want to cry.

"I'm sorry, Honey, if I . . . gave you the wrong . . . idea. I don't . . . lo—" He couldn't finish. Something within him rebelled, and that scared him more than anything else. Without another word, he spun away and unlocked the door, practically yanking it off its hinges.

As he left the hangar, he saw the approaching storm clouds. A shudder of apprehension gripped his stomach and a cold sweat broke out on his forehead. It was the perfect ending to his day, as if he didn't have enough problems.

Honey stared at the open doorway for a full minute before she moved to shut and lock it. She didn't want to be bothered at the moment.

When she turned back to her office, memories of the past hour flooded her mind, and she realized she couldn't stay. She had no idea why Cord had run, unless it was because she had admitted she loved him. Perhaps he didn't want to love again. But at least he hadn't said he didn't love her, and he hadn't said he couldn't love her. That was something. But dammit, why had he run? They could have talked. At least then she would know what he was feeling, what he was thinking.

Shaking her head, Honey unlocked the door and left the office, heading out of the hangar. She had to go home. She had to get control of herself. And most of all, she had to find a way to talk to Cord before he ran away from the airshow completely.

As she climbed into her van and gunned the motor, she didn't pay any attention to the dark clouds moving silently across the once-blue sky. The clouds were creeping in, attempting to blanket the sunlight and shroud the earth in misty veils of darkness. At that moment, she could have cared less. With a final look at Cord's RV, she sped out of the lot toward home.

Cord turned away from the unopened whiskey bottle and looked out into the raging storm. Sheets of water poured from the sky, and the wind whipped the tall sea oats back and forth, imitating the rippling dance of the sea. It was the first storm he'd been through where he didn't feel the need for a drink.

He only hoped Ronnie and Matt had made it to Matt's house before the storm hit. They had been the last to leave, and Ronnie had silently watched Cord as if he'd rather stay. But Cord knew Ronnie needed to be around other people, even if Ronnie didn't.

Lately, Cord had realized just how much he'd taken Ronnie's presence for granted. Ronnie was a good friend; a man couldn't ask for better. But Ronnie needed to get out and make a life for himself. Taking care of a thirty-one-year-old guilt-ridden man for over a year was no life for Ronnie. Funny, but Cord had never even questioned the way they lived until he met Honey. He wasn't the same man he'd been two months ago, and he knew Ronnie needed to get on with his life and find a purpose to it.

With a sigh, Cord leaned over to look out the windshield, and then blinked in surprise. Lightning flashed, revealing a small form staggering toward the hangar, arms wrapped around itself. And then it was gone, swallowed up by the rain and darkness.

"Damn!"

Cord quickly opened the door, and almost had it yanked from his hands as the wind caught it. He closed the door and headed for the place he'd last seen the figure. Before taking two steps, he was soaked to the skin.

As he reached the hangar, he collided with an object. Unable to keep his balance, they both hit the wet, sandy ground. Silently, he cursed and stood, pulling the shivering form up with him. Lightning flashed and he automatically looked down.

"Honey? My God, Honey!"

Cord pulled her closer before they were once again plunged into darkness. He cradled her against his side, rubbing her arms, which felt like solid blocks of ice. As they stumbled back to the RV, he half lifted, half dragged her inside before pulling the door closed behind them.

"Are you okay?"

Shaking, water pouring down her soaking-wet body, Honey jerked her head from side to side, her teeth chattering too much to talk.

"I . . . I . . ." Honey gasped, her normal, sexy little voice now harsh and rasping.

Cord frowned as he turned away to yank some towels from the closet and pull her further into the RV. Standing her on the vinyl kitchen floor, he wrapped one towel around her hair, squeezing the water from her thick braid and rubbing her scalp. Cord felt fear clawing his stomach.

He had to get her warm. Questions could come later, after she wasn't in danger of catching pneumonia.

Quickly, he dried her face and neck, and his eyes briefly met hers before he dropped his gaze to follow the motion of the towel. Her eyes looked so wide, almost feverish. She looked lost, and Cord's heart twisted in silent pain.

"I've got to get you warm. You're freezing to death," he muttered worriedly. He rubbed the towel over her hands, bringing the blood back into them, and then he handed her another towel.

"Keep drying yourself, and get your clothes off," Cord ordered gently. He turned away and rummaged through the closet's drawers, removing a T-shirt and flannel shirt of Ronnie's. Though taller than Cord, Ronnie was leaner.

Cord heard her wet things hit the tile, and he turned with the clothes in his hands, trying to be impersonal. But when he saw her, he hesitated.

She had wrapped a towel around herself, and even with a wet, straggly braid and her hair sticking out at odd angles, she was lovely. She was also trembling with cold.

"Here, get into these while I get dry and change." Cord grabbed more towels and clothes from the closet. Standing in the hall, he dried himself quickly and began slipping into another pair of jeans and a light-blue shirt, all the while muttering to himself. "Damn fool, if you had the hot water fixed, she wouldn't be in danger of freezing to death."

Just the thought was enough to chill him anew. He spun around to find her still standing where he'd left her, Ronnie's Nuke the Whales T-shirt and his red flannel shirt reached her knees. Smiling tenderly, he moved around her and pulled a blanket from Ronnie's bed. He bundled her into it and settled her on the couch like a tiny, cocooned baby.

"You stay here while I dump the wet stuff into the shower and put some coffee on. Okay?"

Taking her jerky nod as agreement, he moved away. After depositing the wet clothes and towels in the bathroom, he turned back to the kitchen and saw the whiskey bottle. He quickly broke the seal and poured a shot into the glass.

"Maybe this'll work better than coffee." Cord sat down beside her and began coaxing her to drink it. Eventually, she downed the whiskey, but she was still shivering, seeming unable to get warm.

Cord set the glass aside and pulled her against his chest, rubbing her arms and back. He tried to get hold of the fear gripping him, but until he got her warm, he knew it wasn't going to go away.

"Do you want to tell me why you were out walking in this mess?"

"I . . . h-had a f-flat."

"Another one? Can't you change a tire?" Cord asked in disbelief. He made a mental note to make sure her van had new tires before the week was out.

"Do-Don't be stupid. Of c-course I can. But the m-mechanic used t-the air gun to put . . . the lu-lug nuts on. I cou-couldn't get th-them loo-loose." Taking a shaky breath, Honey was grateful her explanation was over so she didn't have to talk again. She squirmed, trying without success to get warm. Her eyes were doing strange things, like failing to focus. The three-mile hike in the driving rain had already exhausted her, and that whiskey hadn't helped to clear her head.

She hadn't expected Cord to be awake when she'd stumbled through the storm. After what Ronnie had once told her about the way he hated them, she thought he'd be sleeping through it. But instead, there was no sign of her people, or Ronnie. When she'd gotten caught in the storm, with no one else even on the road, all she'd thought of was getting back here, where someone would be able to take her home. Thoughts of Cord hadn't even intruded until the chills started.

And now, here she was, with Cord. She was where she felt safest, but what about him? Did he resent her intrusion? Honey shivered again, but it wasn't as bad as before.

"Come on, Honey. I'm going to put you to bed. This storm looks like one hell of a cloudburst, and it doesn't look as if it'll be letting up anytime soon," Cord said, his cheek resting on top of her head.

"Ssookay," Honey slurred.

Cord stood and pulled her up beside him. He turned off the lights as she shuffled along with him down the narrow hall to his bedroom. He tucked her into his bed and quickly stripped to join her. He pulled the covers around them and moved her blanket aside, shifting her until she lay snuggled against his chest.

While he waited for his warmth to seep into her body, he began smoothing out her braid, separating her hair so it would dry easier. As it dried, the silky strands wrapped around his fingers.

"Cord," she whispered into the darkness.

"Hmm?" he replied, loath to think about anything except the way she felt in his arms, the rightness of having her here with him.

"I love you, Cord," she croaked, the shudders almost completely gone now.

"I know," he murmured back. For long minutes, he lay staring up at the ceiling as it was illuminated by brief flashes of lightning. He felt her relaxing against him, felt her skin warming, and heard her deep, even breathing. She'd fallen asleep, utterly trusting and safe in his arms.

Cord shifted until he could see the beauty of her sleeping face framed by her thick mane of spun-gold hair.

"I love you, too," he whispered as he pulled her closer.

Honey's slumberous brown eyes opened to find Cord beside her, still sleeping. A tender smile curved her lips when she saw the dark stubble covering his jaw, and the relaxed handsomeness of his face. He'd been so sweet, had taken such good care of her last night. Love for him swelled within her, and she reached up to place a kiss on his cheek.

"Cord?" Her soft, scratchy voice showed the damage of her chill the night before.

Cord stirred and shifted, instinctively reaching for Honey. Slowly, his eyes opened and he smiled. "How are you?"

"Fine," she croaked.

"You don't sound it. Let me get you some water." Without waiting for an answer, he moved away from her, got out of bed, naked, and unself-consciously retrieved his jeans from the floor. He slipped into them before leaving the room.

Honey sighed and shifted, sitting up on the bed. She felt sore all over. Moving the blankets aside, she bared her upper thigh to see what she'd done to herself. She saw the small bruises dotting her skin, and she knew they hadn't come from her fight with the tire iron. A deep, indrawn breath from the doorway brought her head up.

She found Cord standing there, a glass of water held in one hand. His jaw was clenched, and his eyes were trained on her bare thighs. Quickly, she pulled the blankets back over herself and smiled up at Cord.

Cord moved to the bed and sat down beside her, absently handing her the water. He moved the blanket away from her legs carefully, to look at the bruises.

Honey almost dropped the water when she felt Cord's

palm on her thigh, felt him fitting his fingertips to the small bruises marring her creamy-smooth skin.

"I did this, didn't I?" he asked, seeing the way his fingers fit perfectly over the marks.

"They did happen yesterday, but . . ."

"I hurt you," he said, cutting her off. "I . . . I'm sorry." Cord's gruff voice was filled with pain and guilt.

Seeing his self-condemnation, Honey couldn't allow him to blame himself. She took a sip of the water to ease the scratchiness in her throat before putting the glass on the bedside table. Then, she reached out, her small, calloused palm resting on his bristly cheek.

"I've always bruised easily, and they don't really hurt." A small secretive smile curved her lips, and she continued even more softly, "Besides, I thoroughly enjoyed getting them."

Cord groaned and leaned forward to place a gentle kiss on her forehead. He had no idea what he'd done to deserve such a beautiful, understanding woman. He was only thankful she was his.

He leaned down and touched his lips to her hip. Then he moved lower, kissing the bruises on her soft thigh. But he didn't stop there. He continued to her inner thigh, where there weren't any bruises. And finally, he reached the warmth of her center, where he placed a longer kiss on the blond curls covering it.

Sucking in her breath, Honey closed her eyes at the pleasure-pain of his touch. She shifted farther down on the bed, aching for him. The pain of his leaving her was like a bad dream, and when she felt him touch her in the most sensitive and intimate of ways, every trace of hurt faded. There was only now, only Cord.

Gently, Cord shifted her on the bed and pushed the blankets away. He moved up to taste her parted lips in a brief kiss, the roughness of his unshaven chin rasping her sensitive skin and drawing a kittenish purr from her throat. Seeing the proud peaks of her breasts straining against the thin T-shirt, his hooded eyes devoured the sight before he took one cloth-covered peak into his mouth, then moved to the other, pulling gently.

Honey's hands lifted and her fingers dug into his shoulders, her breasts swelling to meet him. "Cord. Oh, Cord . . . please," she rasped.

"Please what?" he whispered, his eyes running over the flushed cheeks, tumbled hair, and half-closed eyes of the woman he loved. Her eyes revealed a passionate, sexy fire that sent flames shooting through his blood stream. She loved him, only him.

"Please . . . *me*."

A shudder swept his entire body at her soft, intimate demand.

"Yes," he whispered in promise.

He slipped out of his jeans, and within moments of joining her on his bed, she was naked and pressed against him. But this time, as his body merged with hers, he lost a part of himself, forever.

Honey watched Ronnie enter the RV and freeze in the doorway. Seeing the shocked expression on his face, she had to keep from laughing by biting the inside of her lip. From her place at the dinette table, she sent him a smile of welcome before returning her attention to her coffee.

"Hi, half-pint. Uh, my clothes don't do a heck of a lot for you," he remarked as he settled down across from her at the table.

"I know, but mine got wet in the storm last night," she returned, her voice still hoarse.

"Sounds like that wasn't the worst of it. Where's Cord?"

"Shaving."

"Uh, the guys were worried when they called and couldn't get you. They drove out toward your place and found your van. Billy Joe stayed with it to fix the tire and bring it back. You'll, uh, probably want someone to tell them you're okay," Ronnie offered.

Honey looked up to find a peculiar expression on Ronnie's face, but she was grateful for his implied offer.

"I'd appreciate it if you'd do that."

"Sure." Rising, he turned away then turned back. "Are you okay?"

"Yes, Ronnie, I'm fine."

Honey watched Ronnie through the window as he headed toward the hangar and a gentle smile lit her face. Next to the guys in her show, he was the closest thing to a brother she had, and it was so obvious he cared. Perhaps the only one it wasn't obvious to was Ronnie. He seemed determined to play the macho, I-don't-need-anybody rebel.

"Why so thoughtful?" Cord questioned as he left the bathroom, a towel draped over his shoulders.

"Just thinking about Ronnie. Sometimes he tries not to show how much he cares," Honey returned. Looking up at Cord, she couldn't keep the love she felt from shining in her eyes, but it didn't seem to bother him.

"Self-defense probably. He had a rough time growing up." Cord shrugged. Then he leaned down and kissed her. "But right now, I really don't want to talk about Ronnie, unless it's to say how glad I am he wasn't here last night, or this morning."

A banging on the RV's door broke them apart, and, with a muttered curse, Cord moved to see who it was. Matt stood outside, a scowl on his weathered face.

"Honey in there?" he questioned gruffly.

"Yes," Cord returned calmly.

Honey stepped up beside Cord, looking like a refugee

in Ronnie's jeans and T-shirt. "Hi, Matt, what can I do for you?"

"You okay, Honey?" Matt's gaze swept over her face and the emotions it revealed, as well as the borrowed clothes she wore.

"I'm fine." Honey smiled. She stepped out of the RV and looked up into Matt's lined face. "Everything's okay," she murmured, feeling Cord's presence behind her as he stepped down to join her.

"Just checkin'." Matt turned away, looking toward the van that was being driven up to the hangar. "You'll be wantin' to go home and change. I'll tell the others you'll be in later," he mumbled, beginning to move away.

"Thanks, Matt."

"Oh, uh, Honey, Pete finally popped the question to Sally. He won't be in today." Matt turned back to Honey, obviously not knowing where to look.

"That's wonderful, Matt. Is there anything else?" she prompted, sensing the older man wasn't ready to leave yet, no matter how much he might want to.

"Rudy wanted to know if you could fill in on the free-fall practice for next week's show. I'll tell him to ask when you get back," he blurted out. Matt began moving away, having done his duty.

Honey smiled fondly before calling out. "Tell him that'll be fine, Matt. I'll be back as soon as I can." She knew it wouldn't be easy for them to accept her relationship with Cord, but she had no intention of hiding it.

With a sigh, she turned to Cord, ready to laugh with him over Matt's obvious discomfort. Only Cord wasn't in a laughing mood. In fact, the man she'd spent the early morning with was gone. In his place was a stranger with shuttered eyes and an expressionless face.

_____ TWELVE _____

As Honey drove back to the hangar, she couldn't help but wonder about Cord. One moment he'd been playful and tender, and the next, he'd frozen up like a TV dinner. He wouldn't even tell her why. She had followed him back into the RV to get her keys and wallet, and all he could say was she needed to get home, shower, and change. He'd bundled her wet clothes into a plastic bag, shuttled her out of the motor home, and shut the door behind her. If it hadn't been for the fact that he was right, she would have started beating on the door and demanded some answers. But she hadn't wanted to give her well-meaning friends and co-workers anything to worry about.

And then again, perhaps Cord just needed some time to think. Their morning together had been beautiful. Then, he had pulled away again. As soon as she got to the hangar, she intended to have a long talk with Cord.

Honey pulled the van into the hangar lot, turned it off, and jumped out with a spring in her step. She came around the back of the van, looked toward the RV, and froze. She saw Cord and Ronnie securing the storage bins. She only hoped it didn't mean what she thought it did.

Reaching the RV, she clasped her trembling hands behind her back and smiled brightly, hoping Cord wouldn't see how strained the smile truly was.

"What's up?" she caroled with forced gaiety.

Ronnie looked up, then ducked his head.

"We're going to be heading out soon," Cord returned without facing her.

"How soon?" she asked brightly.

"About fifteen minutes or so." With his back to her, Cord didn't see the way she flinched.

"Where to?" Strained and hurting, Honey valiantly fought to keep it from her voice.

"Maryland. Home, I guess." He shrugged, turning to lean against the side of the RV. "It's time."

Ronnie disappeared around the back of the motor home, giving them some degree of privacy.

"What about the show . . . ?" Honey began, desperately trying to find a reason that would give her more time, give *them* more time. What had happened this morning? What had she done?

"You'll be fine now. You'll have a handle on everything if you ever get your office clean. I'll have the main office send a good manager down, to help you train for the first month or so."

"Why can't you do that . . . ?" Honey began, only to stop when he shook his head.

"You know why," he stated with a direct look into her eyes.

Yes, she knew why. It was because she'd fallen in love with him. And she could only assume he was leaving to keep from telling her he couldn't love her in return. In fact, leaving probably amounted to the same thing. Pain lanced through her heart. How could she have known his leaving would hurt this bad?

"I'm sorry, Honey. I'm sorry I just couldn't . . ." He

turned away without finishing, pushing his hands into the front pockets of his faded jeans.

Sorry for what; for not being able to love her? What had it been when he cradled her in his arms, stroked her hair, kissed her brow? And what about the time they'd laughed as they watched dolphins from the deck of her beach house, or the times they'd talked long into the night after dinner? What had all that been if not growing love? Could she really have spent weeks deluding herself?

"Well, I'll wish you a safe trip then, and say good-bye now." Honey hid her emotions from him, trying desperately not to let him see the wrenching pain that threatened to break her.

"Yes, well . . . good-bye, Honey," Cord returned. Without another word, he disappeared into the RV.

She wanted to be numb, but she wasn't. Blinking the tears away, she moved around the back of the RV, looking for Ronnie. She stumbled into Ronnie's outstretched arms and couldn't maintain the facade any longer. She clutched his waist, her body convulsing in pain.

Ronnie stroked her hair, his usually guarded blue eyes growing moist with emotion. "Easy, Honey, easy," he crooned softly.

Gasping, Honey refused to let her tears fall. She nodded in small jerks and straightened, holding Ronnie in loving arms.

"Please take care of him for me," she breathed softly, her cheek pressed to Ronnie's lean chest.

"I will," he vowed.

Stepping up on tiptoe, Honey touched his jaw, bringing his head down. She kissed him on the cheek and stepped away, her shoulders squared and her hands balled into fists that she shoved into her pockets.

"I love you, Ronnie. You're the brother I never had, and I'll always be here if you need me." Turning away, not able to watch them leave without crumbling, Honey slowly walked back to the hangar.

Ronnie sniffed and rubbed his aching eyes. Watching her walk away, he couldn't bring himself to move. She was dwarfed by the gigantic building, and she looked all the more lost, all the more alone.

"Damn!" he cursed, closing his eyes tightly.

"Come on, Ronnie. We've got to get a move on," Cord called.

"Yeah," Ronnie snapped.

Entering the RV, Ronnie went to the kitchenette and pulled a soda from the refrigerator. "You're drivin'," he growled belligerently and sprawled onto one of the stuffed chairs.

Cord scowled at Ronnie's uncharacteristic behavior and settled into the driver's seat. He ignored the sudden aching emptiness that assailed him.

Breathing deeply, knowing it was for the best, he started the engine and pulled away from the hangar. Cord knew he was leaving a part of himself with Honey, probably the best part, but he also knew he couldn't bear to watch her constantly risk her life. The airshow was a big part of Honey. She wouldn't give up skydiving, no matter how much it tore him apart. And what of the other dangerous stunts she would do in the future? He couldn't bear to lose the woman he loved, not twice in one lifetime. It was time to go home.

In the days after Cord left, Honey found herself cleaning her office to within an inch of its life. Anything, just to keep busy enough not to think about *him*. But eventually the office was clean, and she could sit behind her desk and see everything the way Cord had wanted it. It made her more depressed than ever. As a result, she spent most of her time outside the hangar.

When she went home, even her beach house gave her no pleasure. It seemed so plain, even worse than before. Now, it was oddly lifeless. The beach house reminded her of Cord and Ronnie, of the times they had teased her, of all the ways they had found to inundate her with knick-knacks and pictures and plants. There would be no more cute little stuffed bears on her dinner plate.

Life was moving on around her. Their next show was less than a week away. Pete and Sally had set the date for their wedding. The new people were becoming part of the "family," and the show was shaping up, if their practice sessions were any indication. Everything she thought she had wanted was happening, but it gave her little pleasure.

Now that she didn't have to worry about money, or about her show, she found she wasn't content. There was no one to share her triumphs with.

Honey stood looking out over her runway. In the distance, she saw three of her pilots practicing their precision flying. She should be happy. Cord was gone, had been gone for three days already, and she'd survived worse things.

"Honey . . ." a voice began from behind her.

Honey spun at the sound of a husky male voice. When she saw Billy Joe, the hope that had flared in her eyes faded, leaving them bleak and lifeless once more.

"Damn, don't be lookin' like that. The sparkle's gone out of you since he left," Billy Joe complained as he leaned against the hangar door.

"What can I do for you, Billy Joe?"

"You can talk to me, for one thing, or to any of us for that matter. Shoot, for three days you've been cleaning that office or wandering around like you were lost. Don't you think we're worried about you? Don't you think we care?" he questioned, letting his irritation show.

"Why'd you get singled out? Diplomacy was never

your strong point," Honey returned. A brief smile lifted the corners of her lips, but it didn't reach her eyes.

"I decided to talk to you before I fly out to pick up those parts. Everybody else is too busy tiptoeing around trying not to upset you. You ain't the first woman to love who didn't get loved back, you know?"

Honey flinched, and his anger evaporated. He began cursing, not even bothering to excuse himself.

"I'm sorry."

"No, you're right." Honey shrugged her slim shoulders and looked back out over the runway.

"Well, hell! Ain't you even going to tell me off for cussin'?"

"Nope."

"Honey, snap out of it! For Pete's sake, is he worth this? You wasn't even this bad when Andy died," Billy Joe growled in frustration.

Honey spun around, her eyes lit with anger. "Yes, he's worth it. I love him. He's one hell of a special man, and don't you forget it! I can't help it that you never tried to get along with him. That's your problem. But I won't hear anything against Cord. And as far as Andy is concerned, you said it—he's dead. He would have been happy I found someone to love, someone to spend my life with." Honey's voice was harsh, her emotions close to the surface, too close.

"I know that, Honey. And if I could, I'd haul Cord back and tie him to a plane for you." Billy Joe smiled, trying to encourage her to do the same.

A reluctant smile lit her face briefly, and the anger drained away.

"I just want you to see that you got a life even though he ain't in it."

"Thanks, Billy Joe," Honey murmured. This time

when she turned away, Billy Joe just faded back into the hangar.

She didn't have to worry about Billy Joe anymore. The increase in salary had changed him. When she'd asked what the problem had been, he'd finally told her. Even working two jobs, he'd been in danger of losing his house. She'd often seen Cord watching Billy Joe, and she knew he had been worried that Billy Joe would hurt the show. Too bad she couldn't explain it all to Cord. Too bad he hadn't stayed long enough to see the change in Billy Joe.

With a sigh, Honey realized Billy Joe was right. There was no sense wandering around and making everyone miserable, including herself, just because her heart was broken.

Suddenly, she felt a sharp pang of homesickness. She wanted to see her folks. There was no reason why she couldn't. All she had to do was fly out to the Blue Ridge and call them when she got there. It would be so wonderful to see them, to be held in her mom's comforting embrace, to have her dad tell her everything was going to work out fine.

"You are the stupidest, stubbornest, most hard-headed son of a—"

"Just leave me alone, Ronnie. I'm not in the mood, okay."

Flinging himself onto the couch, Ronnie stared up at the paneled ceiling in obvious frustration.

Cord sank deeper into the stuffed chair and glared at his cup of coffee. His father had been happy to see him; so had Antony for that matter. They'd welcomed him back as though he'd merely been on vacation. If there was a certain sadness in Antony's eyes when he thought Cord wasn't looking, well, that was to be expected. Going home hadn't been as bad as Cord thought it would be. There was only one problem: he wasn't needed there. His father had stepped into his place and filled it admirably.

Cord hadn't stayed at the airfield, or in Maryland, for more than two days. But, for once, he didn't have anywhere to go. The only place he wanted to go was the one place he couldn't. That hadn't stopped him from heading south again, and, as usual, Ronnie had insisted on tagging along. They were close enough to the North Carolina border to spit.

"You want to know what she said before we left?"

"Ronnie, I told you I didn't want to talk about her, and I meant it," Cord threatened.

"Tough. You were the one that ran away. Again," Ronnie said in disgust.

"Just leave it!" Cord had been refusing for the four days since they'd left North Carolina to discuss Honey. He'd done everything he could to avoid it, even fixed the hot water tank. Just the thought of her brought a sharp pain to his chest. He couldn't bear to talk about her, to hear her name.

"She made me promise something before we left," Ronnie said softly, trying a gentler approach.

Curiosity got the best of him. As much as he didn't want to hear it, Cord had to know what she'd made Ronnie promise.

"What?" Cord asked, not even looking at Ronnie. He set his coffee cup on the small table beside him and leaned forward, his arms resting on his knees.

"She said, 'Please take care of him for me.' "

"Oh, God!" Cord groaned, covering his face with hands that shook. He'd hurt her and still she thought of him first.

"We goin' back?" Ronnie asked cautiously.

"No. I told you, Ronnie, it's better this way."

"Hell! Just who's it better for? Not her. You had it all,

and you were just to damned full of the past to reach out and take it. Oh, you took what she offered all right, and you knew she offered it out of love. But instead of leavin' her alone, like you should have, you took her, and then you up and left. She *loved* you!"

"Do you think I don't know that? Do you think it was easy to leave her? I love her, too!" Cord cried in anguish.

Ronnie sprang to a sitting position on the couch. His jaw dropped open in surprise as he looked at Cord.

"You love her?"

Cord sank back against the chair. "Yes," he sighed tiredly.

"And you left her anyway?" Ronnie questioned in disbelief.

"Don't you think it hurts? There hasn't been an hour that I haven't thought of her. But I couldn't stay. I just couldn't."

"Why?"

"Because I couldn't stand to watch her risk her life every time she jumped out of a plane. I couldn't stand seeing her take those kind of chances at the air show. My fear would have eventually destroyed me, and her," Cord explained, his voice dull and lifeless.

Ronnie sat in silence for a moment before looking at Cord strangely.

"Do you think by not bein' there to watch that she won't be doin' it anyway? What's to keep her from slippin' in the tub and breaking a leg? She could be hurt anytime, doin' anything. Bein' afraid of her job is crazy. If it was me, I'd be there to make sure she didn't do fool stupid things. Nobody can keep someone from bein' hurt, but you can be there for them. You just ran away again, and this time just because you figured you might lose her like you lost Gina." Ronnie shook his head sadly.

Cord froze as Ronnie's words penetrated his pain. He

realized he didn't know what Honey was doing right this minute. He didn't know what was happening to her. No one would tell him if she needed him because they didn't even know he cared!

He'd been there for her that night at the tavern, when they first met. If nothing else, that night proved she had a penchant for getting into trouble. He'd been there the day she almost floated out to sea. She could have died, but that knowledge hadn't sent him running.

That night when she practically froze in the storm, he'd cared for her. Was she even now sick with pneumonia? He hadn't stayed around long enough to find out.

And now, what if Phesner had ignored the warning Cord gave him before he left North Carolina? Was he bothering Honey again? Did she need him?

Lord, Ronnie was right. He had realized he loved her, and he'd run. This time, he hadn't run from the past, but from the uncertainty of the future. But being apart from her, wondering what was happening, if she needed him, would turn his life into absolute hell.

She was a professional. For a while, he'd allowed himself to forget that fact. However, accidents happened. She might die, and he'd never know. All he'd feel was an emptiness, as if he'd lost the best part of himself. He couldn't live that way, he couldn't. He was incomplete without her. He needed her, maybe even more than she needed him.

"Ronnie, I've been a fool," Cord whispered.

It all came down to taking a chance. If he took a chance on their love, at least they'd be together, and they could share their time together, however long it was, making each second count. He could bask in Honey's love and shower her with his own. They could talk and laugh and cry together, make love, and maybe he would be lucky enough to see her body swell with his child.

There were no guarantees, but it was the quality that counted, not the quantity. Remembering Gina, as he hadn't done since the accident, reinforced that belief. Their time had always been special, the memories something to be cherished. He'd thrown it all away out of fear.

He had to go back. He had to try. Being without Honey now, like this, wasn't making him happier. It was only when he was with her that he truly felt alive. The time he spent with her had made him the happiest he had ever been. With Honey, he had finally started to feel whole again. With her, he had a chance to love again.

And he had run away.

Well, he was going to run one last time, but this time, he was going to run *to* Honey.

Straightening with new determination, Cord looked up to find Ronnie waiting.

"Let's go home, Ronnie."

"Hot damn!" Ronnie laughed as he sprang toward the driver's seat.

He started the engine while Cord put away their coffee cups.

"How do you feel about a promotion?" Cord asked from the kitchen area.

Ronnie turned in the plush driver's seat and just stared at Cord in question.

Cord looked up and shrugged. "I figure you could handle my end of things, tour around and inspect businesses, or you can stay with Honey and me. Your choice."

"I ain't educated enough, and she won't be wanting me hanging around forever," Ronnie replied shortly, turning back to lock his seat in position.

Cord took the passenger seat and sighed. "You're educated, and you're intelligent. If you ever decide to drop the juvenile delinquent act, you'll make a damn good businessman. As for Honey, we'll have to see."

Ronnie didn't reply. Instead, he turned the radio on, tuning it until he found a rock-music station.

"What about Leland and Antony?" Ronnie asked, over the radio's music.

"I'll call Dad and Antony on the mobile phone and invite them to the wedding," Cord replied, dropping the subject of Ronnie's future . . . for the moment.

Ronnie put the motor home in gear and the news came on the radio. Ronnie reached automatically to turn down the volume. Cord grabbed Ronnie's hand, his grip painful as the voice on the radio said the few words guaranteed to rivet Cord's attention.

". . . In other news, late yesterday afternoon, a plane went down in the Blue Ridge mountain area of North Carolina. Rescuers are still searching, but have been unable to locate the crash site. A spokesman at the Johnson Airshow refused to identify the pilot until the family has been notified . . ."

The RV pitched forward as Ronnie slammed the brake pedal to the floor. Cord's blood turned to ice in his veins. Looking up, his eyes met Ronnie's. Their fear was a tangible thing in the silence of the motor home. A feeling of déjà vu struck Cord, and in the grip of heart-rending despair, his eyes closed, and his tortured voice rasped through the stillness.

"Dear God, no!" he cried in anguish. "I can't lose her now!"

The large motor home ripped out of the grocery store parking lot, straight into traffic, leaving blaring horns behind as it sped down the street. Cord reached for the mobile phone, his hand trembling.

THIRTEEN

The RV screeched to a halt at the small airfield outside of Marion, North Carolina. Cord jumped out and headed for the half-dozen men clustered near a large blue-and-white helicopter. He searched frantically for Honey, and his fear mounted. He didn't see her anywhere.

After Kelly, the new balloonist at the airshow, had given him directions and a phone number for the rescue operation headquarters, Cord had spent a frustrating few hours trying to get more information. No one he spoke to would release the identity of the pilot.

Kelly had told him both Honey and Billy Joe had taken planes out the day before, heading for the Blue Ridge Mountains, but she didn't know who had gone down. Cord had been unable to get through to any of the airshow personnel helping with the search. He only knew the downed plane hadn't been found yet. The thought of Honey, hurt and alone, up in the mountains, made his chest tighten.

His nerves were shot. Where was Honey? Was she up on the side of some damn mountain? He didn't think he could bear it if anything happened to her.

"Who the hell was involved in the crash?" Cord shouted the question as he approached the men, his voice carrying to them through the sound of the rising wind.

One older man turned and frowned at Cord. "Just who are you, mister?"

"Cord Wayne, part owner of the Johnson Airshow," Cord replied, reining in his temper. He knew anger wouldn't get him answers.

"Well, I don't . . ."

"Cord!"

Cord spun around, searching for the owner of that beautiful, familiar voice. He saw Honey hurrying toward him from a small building to his right. Everything else faded to insignificance. Cord had eyes only for Honey. She was safe.

He met her halfway and swept her into his arms, holding her tightly. The wind swirled around them, kicking up dust, but Cord only cared about the feel of Honey pressed against him. He could feel each breath she took. She was alive. Silently, he offered a prayer of thanks. He blindly searched for her lips. He kissed her hungrily, allowing all the pent-up worry and love to pour out of him. He had been afraid he'd lost her forever.

Cord heard the rough clearing of a throat and reluctantly eased away from Honey. He kept one arm wrapped around her. Looking down, he saw the dark circles under her eyes, the hollowness of her cheeks. She looked as though she'd lost weight. Her eyes never left his face, and he offered her a tender, encouraging smile and squeezed her waist.

"She okay?" Ronnie asked.

Turning, Cord saw Ronnie waiting patiently, his blue eyes trained on Honey.

"Why not ask her?" Cord replied. Now that he had

Honey in his arms, his tension and strain were melting away.

Honey's gaze left Cord's beloved face reluctantly. She needed Cord's strength so much right now, and he'd come. When she saw Ronnie, saw his concern for her, she instinctively reached out and laid her hand on his arm.

"I'm fine. It's good to see you again, Ronnie," she said, her voice soft.

Ronnie grinned. "It's good to see you, too, half-pint."

Cord heard a shout and commotion behind them. Reality returned. Honey was safe, but one of his people was still in trouble.

"Was it Billy Joe who went down, Honey?" he questioned, his eyes searching her face, seeing the sorrow and worry clouding her dark eyes.

"Yes," she replied in a subdued voice, confirming what he already knew.

Cord tightened his hold on her when he felt her tremble. Turning her back into his arms, he began rocking her in a soothing motion, holding her close and stroking her back.

"Where's his family?"

"I couldn't tell Evelyn. She's already having trouble with her pregnancy, and the doctor said she might not carry this one to term. I . . . I couldn't upset her, not yet, not till we know something. They almost lost their house, and now this. I didn't want to worry her. The waiting has been hell, Cord. I wanted to spare her," she explained softly.

He didn't know that he agreed with her logic, but she knew Billy Joe's wife better than he did. Perhaps it was best to keep her out of it for now. Honey obviously needed assurance that she'd made the right decision. He knew he would always stand by her, and that was all that mattered now.

"It's okay, Honey. Why don't we go see if anything is happening?" He guided her back to the cluster of men, with Ronnie following silently behind them. Cord saw Matt and Rudy had joined the other men, and something was causing a stir.

"Matt . . ." Cord began, drawing the older man's attention. Matt nodded a greeting and stepped away from the other men.

"The Civil Air Patrol just located the plane, Cord. It's in the mountains, up in the Pisgah National Forest."

"Why the hell isn't the chopper going out?"

"There's a storm coming in. An inexperienced man can't go up in a helicopter in this weather. With the winds the way they are, and night coming on, it'd be suicide. We have a professional rescue team on the way. We're waitin' on them now," Matt replied.

"We're gonna have to keep waitin', Cord. There ain't nothing we can do until the rescue team gets here." Pete ducked his head, not wanting anyone to see the worry he was trying to hide. Sally stood next to him, her hand on his arm, offering him support. Rudy, Pete, and Sally had all flown out as soon as the search started for the downed plane.

Cord paid no attention to Pete's words. He turned away and searched the darkening sky. "Where are the maps?"

Rudy led the way to the small building near the helicopter. He produced the maps Cord wanted and spread them out over a small rickety table.

Honey stood close to Cord's side, her arm wrapped around his waist. Having him to lean on made her feel stronger. He was back, and for now, that was enough.

Cord looked over the map, absently running his hand up and down Honey's back as he listened to the men explain where they'd finally spotted Billy Joe's plane before high winds had forced them to return to the airfield.

Cord then listened to the weather forecast and the men's predictions.

He loosened his hold on Honey and slipped away, leaving the men to mill around and wait for the weather to clear, or the rescue team to get there. He walked outside, tucked his hands into the front pockets of his jeans, and looked northwest, toward the mountains where Billy Joe's plane had gone down. He felt the cool bite of the wind buffet against his body, and looked again to the menacing bank of storm clouds that were getting closer.

"What's wrong, Cord?" Honey asked as she came up behind him. She shivered at the chill that seeped through her dark-blue sweatshirt and jeans.

"I don't like waiting and doing nothing. We have to get to him. He's got a wife and kids," Cord said. Cord had no intention of telling Billy Joe's family that he wouldn't be coming home again, not unless he'd done everything in his power to turn things around.

"Cord . . ." Honey began softly, moving forward to wrap her arms around his waist from behind. She laid her cheek against his back and felt the tension in him. "The rescue team should be here soon."

"I don't intend to wait. Where's the owner of the blue-and-white helicopter?"

"Inside, but what . . . ?"

Cord stepped away and turned to face her. Looking down, he tried to maintain a certain air of authority for her benefit.

"I'm going to go up and get Billy Joe, if I can."

"I'll go with you," Honey said without hesitation.

"No!" Cord snapped. The piercing fear that shot through his heart almost took his breath away.

"Why not? You'll need some help." She didn't want to let him out of her sight, and she didn't want him facing danger alone.

"Honey . . ." Cord's voice was raspy with emotion. "Honey, I couldn't function if you were out there." Cord's hands went to her shoulders as he tried to make her understand. His worry and fear made his statement harsher than he had intended it to be.

She understood. He didn't want her with him. And maybe he was right. She'd been awake for over twenty-four hours already. She would probably be a hindrance to him, but she still didn't want to see him go alone. He needed someone to take care of him, to make sure he took care of himself.

"Okay, Cord, but please take someone else. You'll need . . ." She stopped talking when she heard the sound of a helicopter cut through the sound of the wind.

Cord moved away from Honey as the helicopter landed.

A lean blond man in a green khaki flight suit stepped out of the helicopter and started walking toward them. Cord moved forward to meet him.

"Josh Andrews of Andrews Search and Rescue," the man said, stopping to offer his hand to Cord.

"Cord Wayne," Cord responded, shaking Josh's hand.

"Of Wayne and Cray?" Josh asked. He received a nod from Cord in answer. "What's the situation?" Josh questioned respectfully.

"Are you ready to take off?"

"My partner, Lee Kane, is refueling. We'll be ready once he's done."

"I'm going with you," Cord stated.

"I don't advise it, sir."

"One of my people is on that mountain. I'm going to do whatever I can to help get him home safely."

Josh gave Cord a long, measuring look, then nodded. "Let's get underway."

Cord turned back to find Honey watching him, her eyes wide, her teeth worrying her lower lip.

"Don't worry, Honey, everything will work out just fine."

"You be careful, okay?"

"Sure." Cord gave her a quick, hard kiss and turned away. He didn't see Ronnie come up and join Honey.

Josh and Cord headed for the helicopter, with Cord talking as they went. "He went down yesterday. The crash wasn't spotted until today, before the weather forced the search teams in."

Josh nodded as Cord gave him the coordinates. Josh then took his place in the right pilot's seat. Les took the left. As the two men went through their checks, Cord strapped himself into one of the seats in the back.

When the door opened and Ronnie climbed in the back with him, Cord turned to him in disbelief.

"What the hell do you think you're doing?" Cord snapped.

Ronnie shrugged. "We all gotta face fear sometime."

"Not today you don't. Get out of here. I don't want to be worrying about you, too."

"Tough. Honey was upset, and I made a promise to her a while back. She wanted to come so she could look out for you. Since she said you didn't want her, I decided to tag along and keep an eye on you."

"Ronnie, dammit!"

"You're wasting time. Let's get moving."

"Then get out."

"No."

"All right, I'll put you out."

Ronnie faced him, meeting Cord's fury with his own. "I care about Honey, Cord, and I'm going to make sure the two of you get a second chance. I'm going to keep you safe for her, and I'm not getting out without a fight."

"Either we take off now or we won't get him off that mountain tonight," Josh called back to them.

Defeated, Cord turned to Josh. "Let's go," he said before putting on one of the extra headsets and motioning for Ronnie to do the same.

When they took off to a hover, the force of the wind pushed against the helicopter, sending it swooping sideways. As the helicopter fought the elements, Cord's thoughts turned back to Honey. Why did she tell Ronnie that he didn't want her? What had he said to make her think that?

It was Ronnie who first saw the wreckage. Though a little pale, and more than a little shaken, Ronnie was holding up through sheer willpower. When he spotted the downed plane, he tapped Cord's shoulder, pointing. Cord shook off his thoughts of Honey and turned his mind to the task at hand.

The terrain was almost all forest, with rocky cliffs and deep gorges. Cord had no idea how they'd reach Billy Joe in this weather, not if they had to use the hoist mounted on the right side of the helicopter.

Josh's resonant voice came over the headset. "It looks like we're in luck. It appears there's a grassy bald on this mountaintop, probably what he was heading for. Let's hope it *is* grass and not shrubs. If our luck holds, I can set us down."

Trying to hover with the helicopter was next to impossible. The crosswinds rocked it back and forth like a giant cradle. The bald turned out to be tall grass surrounded by rhododendrons, but there was a large enough space to land. Josh dropped toward it, not all on his own power. The wind helped push him there. Though not the smoothest of landings, at least they were down, and still alive.

"We'll help," Cord stated. He pulled off the headset and jumped out of the helicopter.

"I didn't figure on stopping you. Les will go with you,

and I'll make sure we're ready to take off as soon as you get back.''

Cord gave Josh a thumbs-up and slung a coiled nylon rope over his head and shoulder. Les, a short, stocky older man in a green khaki flight suit, grabbed a communicator and the first aid kit.

Cord, Ronnie, and Les sprinted toward the trees, fighting the wind which alternately tried to push them back and then sweep them forward. Then, it became an exercise to make it through the underbrush and down the steepening slope. When they reached the cliff where the plane had gone down, Cord took in the scene with a growing sense of horror.

The plane had plowed into the trees at the top of a steep incline leading down to a sheer cliff. The cliff overlooked a deep ravine. The plane's wings had snapped off like mere matchsticks. Then, the pull of gravity and the added force of the wind appeared to have pushed the plane back down the incline. It now sat teetering on the cliff's edge, threatening to topple to the rocks far below.

Cord felt an icy shiver in his midsection. If the plane went over before they got him out . . .

Cord pulled the coil of rope over his head. He tossed most of the rope to Les, who had dropped the communicator and first aid kit upon seeing the situation. Cord started to slide and scramble down the rocky incline as Les quickly wrapped the rope twice around a large tree and made sure Cord had enough line to get to the plane. Though he couldn't see anyone inside, Cord knew they had to secure the plane long enough to get the injured man out.

All around him, the deadly storm was worsening.

Reaching the plane, Cord threaded the rope around the bent metal of the propeller blades, trying to steady the wreckage for just a few minutes. The teetering plane, like a gruesome kind of slow-motion seesaw, pulled back, away from the rope, tautening it before Cord could tie a securing knot.

From where he stood, Ronnie saw rocks starting to crumble on the cliff's edge. He sprang forward, grabbing the rope and half falling in his attempt to reach Cord's side.

As the plane slipped, tearing the end of the rope from Cord's palms, Ronnie's hand shot out to grab Cord's belt. Cord lost his footing and almost went down. Ronnie was the only force steadying Cord and keeping him from toppling over the edge of the cliff.

Before their eyes, the plane tilted precariously. More rock gave way, and under the sudden impact of a fresh gust of wind, the plane slid from the cliff, like a beached whale returning to the sea.

Cord's curse broke through the fury of the wind, his voice echoing around the mountain.

An explosion rent the air, followed by billowing, swirling clouds of smoke. Cord turned and fought his way back up the incline, helping Ronnie when the younger man stumbled. Cord was beginning to feel the bleeding rope burns on his palms, but he couldn't afford to worry about them, not now.

When they reached safe ground, Ronnie heaved a giant sigh of relief.

"What now?" Ronnie had to shout to be heard.

Cord just shook his head, his eyes searching for something in the surrounding woods. He wasn't ready to give up, not yet. If Billy Joe had managed to get out of the plane, he might be in the trees. It was the only hope left.

Puzzled, Ronnie stood beside a strangely silent Cord. Les joined them and reached to examine Cord's hands. Cord shook him off and moved to the left, where he thought he saw a vague trail.

The air stilled, in a strange, eerie hush that sometimes precedes a storm. Silence swept across the mountainside.

"What is it? What's wrong?" Ronnie questioned.

"I think there's a trail here. He could have gotten out of the plane."

"The storm . . ." Les began.

"Damn the storm. I'm going down this trail." Cord started off, and both Ronnie and Les followed him.

With a deafening clap of thunder signaling the end to the silent respite, torrential rain poured from the darkened sky,whipped horizontal by the strength of the wind.

All three men slid along the rocks and grass, entering a stand of trees that offered meager protection from the storm. They began searching, and Les branched off in a different direction, following another faint trail.

Cord stumbled through the trees, near where the sheared-off wings had fallen. He moved farther back, following a trail of broken branches. Reaching a large boulder, he stopped and leaned against it. Water dripped from his face, half blinding him.

"Don't you make me have to go back and tell Honey we lost you," Cord muttered as his gaze moved over the surrounding trees, looking for more broken branches. He only hoped Billy Joe had a very tolerant and protective guardian angel.

Pushing away from the rock, he moved to renew his search. Rocks slid under his feet. With a shout, quickly drowned out by the storm's fury, he fell, tumbling into a foliage-covered depression such as a deer might use for her fawn.

His impromptu slide halted when he came up against the warmth of a living creature. Wiping the water from his face, he looked down to find Billy Joe lying silent and still beside him.

"Thank God," Cord said as he felt for, and found, a strong pulse.

Though badly scraped and bruised, Billy Joe appeared to have no broken bones. But he had an egg-size lump on the side of his head. He was wrapped in a silvery space blanket, and Cord hoped it had been enough to protect him from exposure.

"Cord," Ronnie called, pushing aside branches. He poked his head through the ferns and other foliage, and seemed to relax when he saw both Cord and Billy Joe.

"Is he all right?" Ronnie asked.

"I don't know. I think he will be. Get Les, we'll need his help." Ronnie left and the branches fell back into place.

"Hell, does this mean I gotta be nice to you from now on?" Billy Joe croaked. His eyes flickered, and he looked up, trying to focus on Cord.

Cord leaned forward and smiled. "I don't care if you cuss me daily just as long as I get you back to your wife and kids in one piece."

"Good enough," Billy Joe murmured drowsily.

_____ FOURTEEN _____

Honey watched the rhythmic crash of the surf from the deck of her beach house. It was sunset, and inevitably, darkness would come. She knew, just as inevitably, Cord would leave; it was only a matter of time.

Cord had surprised her when he came back to the air-show. She'd thought that once he got Billy Joe off the mountain, he'd take off again. Instead, she had his RV camped by the hangar, as though he'd never left. Since his arrival, he'd made her life easier by handling the media and the insurance companies. But now, there was no reason for Cord to stay.

"Is something wrong?"

She almost sighed when she heard Cord's voice. It still had the power to melt her into a little puddle on the floor. His voice was so beautifully masculine, so deep and sexy. She could easily spend the rest of her life listening to him talk.

"No. I'm fine," she replied without turning around. He was here to tell her he was leaving; she knew it.

Cord stared at her stiff back and his brow arched as he silently questioned her actions. In the past three days, she had managed to avoid him at every turn.

In his mind, he remembered the harrowing helicopter ride; Josh Andrews had more nerve than brains. He remembered Honey's reaction when he stepped off that helicopter. She'd been standing out in the pouring rain, with an older couple who were huddled under a large umbrella. Honey's relief had been obvious. Before he had taken three steps, she was in his arms, kissing him and holding him tight, as if she would never let him go. Then, for no reason, she withdrew completely. Though he'd met and liked her parents, he found Honey used them as a buffer, and he was glad when it was time to return to the coast. But since they had gotten back, whenever he tried to get her alone, she either excused herself, or something "came up" that needed her attention.

Watching the breeze play with the hem of her white crinkle-cotton blouse, Cord felt oddly hesitant. He was unsure of his reception now that he finally had her alone. Had he managed to kill the love she felt for him, or had she only *thought* she loved him?

"Where's Ronnie?" Honey asked, still not turning around.

"He dropped me off and took a drive over to Matt's house for dinner. He'll be back later." Cord didn't tell her he had planned it this way.

"Umm," Honey murmured.

"Do they know why the plane went down?" he asked.

"No. The FAA and National Transportation Safety Board are still investigating. Billy Joe said it was a total system failure. We'll see what the NTSB thinks when we get their report." Honey shrugged. She wasn't worried about the report, not after what Billy Joe had described, and she knew the insurance would cover the cost of the plane.

"How is Billy Joe doing?" Cord moved closer to the weathered wooden rail, and Honey. If he could keep her talking, maybe he could find out what was wrong. Something about her was different, remote. It had to be more than his leaving. At the Marion airfield, she had been so loving, and then she'd changed.

"He's fine. The hospital released him, so he's home now. He won't be flying for a while, but he was lucky to get away with a mild concussion," Honey said. Then, in a more subdued tone, she continued. "He's glad I didn't tell his wife until we knew he was okay, but she hasn't forgiven me yet." Honey sighed and reached up to toss her braid back over her shoulder.

"Honey, you did what you thought best."

"I know. I got to thinking about it last night, while I was visiting them. She finally talked to me, but it wasn't like before. I realized I was wrong to leave her out, and I apologized. Maybe, in time . . ." Honey didn't tell him what had caused her realization. She had thought of Cord, and what she would have felt in the same situation, if someone had kept her from him.

Cord heard the pain in Honey's voice and reached out to lightly grasp her shoulders, pulling her back against his chest.

"It *will* be okay. She'll forgive you for caring too much. Your loving nature isn't a crime, Honey, it's a very special part of you," he murmured close to her ear.

"Thank you, Cord." Her voice was breathless, her body helplessly reacting to his touch.

Honey stepped away from his light hold and turned to face him. Seeing the blatant hunger of Cord's gaze made her catch her breath. Her pulse jumped to life.

"Cord, I . . ." she began, unsure what she was going to say, what she should do. The sound of the surf almost covered her soft, hesitant voice.

He reached up and placed one finger over her lips. "It's okay, Honey." He smiled tenderly, and when he moved his hand away, she caught a glimpse of the healing rope burn on his palm.

"How are your hands?"

Cord looked down at the hand she was staring at so intently. Turning his hand over, palm up, he let her see the damage wasn't too severe.

"They're fine."

She was so glad Ronnie had gone with him. She'd read the report. She knew she'd almost lost Cord, permanently. She wanted to hold his hand, to kiss his palm, cradle it against her cheek and tell him she didn't want him to leave, ever. She knew she couldn't do that. But what would he think if she reached out to him and refused to think of tomorrow in favor of one more night in his arms?

"Cord," she murmured achingly, stepping forward and lifting her hands to link them behind his neck.

Cord didn't question, didn't hesitate. He bent and covered her mouth with gentle mastery. His tongue brushed her lips, parting them, needing to taste the nectar he knew awaited him.

At her soft moan, Cord pulled back. "Honey?" he questioned, sensing something was wrong but not sure what it was.

"I need you, Cord. I want you . . . now. I want you to fill the emptiness . . ." She loved him beyond reason. When he left, she knew he would take her heart. But for now, he was here, holding her. It was enough, it had to be. He would never give her more.

Cord felt a shiver of need course through her body. An answering tremor shook him. Silently, he followed her through one of the sliding-glass doors and found himself in her bedroom.

Honey pulled him forward as she backed toward her quilt-covered brass bed. She stopped beside the bed and reached up, taking his face between her hands and lifting up to kiss him.

He hadn't meant for this to happen so soon, at least not until they had a chance to talk in depth. But when her mouth fused with his, he couldn't summon the will to stop her. Talking would come later. Right now, he needed her. They needed each other.

Cord woke abruptly. He didn't know what had disturbed him until he realized the other side of the double bed was empty. Where was Honey?

Fumbling with the bedside clock, he saw the LED display said 6:00 A.M. He got out of bed, not bothering to turn on the light. He pulled on his jeans and zipped them before he went into the living room. He sensed the house was as empty as the bed had been. Where had she gone?

Cord moved to the sliding-glass door in the dining room, opened it, and went out onto the deck. He glanced up, then down, the beach. In the predawn light, he saw her walking along the shore. She wore jeans and a light-blue jacket to ward off the chill of the early-morning air and the ocean breeze.

Cord quickly retrieved his green sports shirt and slipped it on before leaving the beach house to join Honey. They had spent most of the night making love, and had eventually fallen into a sated, exhausted sleep. Obviously, it was time for them to talk. He had to know what was so wrong it would take her from their bed at such an hour.

Honey moved farther up the beach to the dry sand. She knelt and picked up a handful of sand, then let it sift through her fingers. She couldn't help thinking of an hour-glass; time was running out.

Images flashed through her mind, images of Cord. If she closed her eyes, she could feel his hand stroking her hair, touching her shoulder, her breast, her face. That was one of the many things she loved about him, the way he enjoyed holding her and touching her after they made love. Each time, he always stroked her, calmed her, pleased her. His tenderness, his sharing, his warmth, made her feel so much a woman, so loved. But he didn't love her.

Cord was a magnificently tender, totally masculine man who knew how to treat a woman in the most intimate sense. She had to remember, to understand, their time together didn't mean the same thing to him that it meant to her. She had to accept him the way he was, including the fact he would leave again. She had to block out the unrealistic hopes and dreams of her heart.

"Honey?"

Honey looked up, not surprised to see him standing next to her. She could see the concern darkening his gentle eyes, as well as the questions.

"Hello, Cord." She turned back to watch the ocean and felt him sit down beside her, felt him watching her.

"Dammit, Honey, what's wrong?" Cord asked, his control snapping when she continued to ignore him.

"Nothing."

Cord reached out and grasped her shoulder, turning her, making her face him.

"Let's try this again. Why did you leave our bed?" he questioned, trying to calm down and take things slowly.

"I needed time to think," she replied just as calmly.

She didn't seem like the same Honey he knew and loved. She seemed almost . . . numb.

"Why have you been avoiding me?"

"I haven't. We've both been busy."

"Bull . . ." he began then stopped himself. "Honey, I know what it is to avoid someone. I tried to pull the same stunt with you when I first got here."

Honey's eyes widened in surprise, and Cord could only

hope he was getting through to her. When she didn't say any more, Cord groaned and dropped his hand from her shoulder. He reached up to rub the back of his neck with one hand and looked out toward the horizon.

"I killed it, didn't I? I killed the love you had for me. Oh, the sex is still there, but the rest . . . Do you hate me now?" Cord asked, his voice filled with quiet despair.

Honey felt the numbness wearing off. His pain reached her as nothing else could. She hesitantly touched his forearm, bringing his head around. His gaze met hers.

"I don't hate you, Cord, I never have."

"Then what's wrong? Tell me, please, and I'll fix it."

Honey smiled sadly and shook her head.

"When are you leaving, Cord?" she asked softly, keeping her gaze level and unemotional with an effort.

"When am I . . . ?" Cord's jaw dropped in surprise and dawning realization. "Honey, I'm not leaving."

It was her turn to look at him in shocked surprise. She shook her head, and couldn't help the distressed murmur that escaped her lips.

"But, Cord, I don't understand." She couldn't let herself hope, not yet.

"Honey, how could I leave you? You're the woman who makes me whole, the woman I love, the woman who's going to be my wife?" He offered his heart and waited breathlessly to see if she would accept.

Her lower lip trembled as she looked up and searched his eyes. She didn't have to search hard. She saw the one thing she never expected to see. Love.

"Cord. Oh, Cord." Tears welled in the deep dark brown of her eyes, shimmering on her lashes before spilling down her creamy cheeks. With a soft cry, she scrambled onto his lap, burying her face in the curve of his neck.

Cord gently pushed Honey back, reaching out to lift her

face up to his so he could see her more clearly. He brushed the hair away from her forehead, his touch tender.

"What's wrong, Honey?" He began to kiss the tears away, not understanding their origin.

"I never expected you to love me. When you left, I thought for sure . . ."

"Honey, I do love you. I think I always have. I loved you when I left, but because of your job, I was afraid of losing you, the way I lost Gina, so I ran. That's when I discovered the true meaning of the word *hell*," Cord declared, looking into her eyes, wanting to wipe out the barriers his own fear had built between them. "Can you forgive me for hurting you, Honey?"

He looked so afraid of her answer, and Honey knew then that she would have forgiven him anything, only this time, there was nothing to forgive. Because of his past, she understood what had happened when he realized he loved her. She was only glad he had come back to her.

"Cord, I love you, and there's nothing to forgive. You came back, that's the important thing," she said, reaching out to run her fingers through the wavy dark hair at his nape. "But I do have one question."

"What?" Cord asked. He reached up to stroke her hair, her face. Knowing she still loved him caused a warm glow to spread through his body.

"Why didn't you want me to go in the helicopter with you? I thought it was because you didn't . . . want me," she said, giving voice to the uncertainty that had put a wall between them after the accident.

Now Cord understood what Ronnie had been talking about in the helicopter. Cord supposed he still had a lot to learn about expressing his love and concern to Honey.

"Sweetheart, I'd just driven hundreds of miles to get to you, believing you might have been taken away from me in a plane crash. I was so relieved you were safe, the only thought in my mind was keeping you that way. I didn't want you with me because I knew I'd worry more about you than Billy Joe. Never think I don't want you. I want you more than you can ever know." His hands continued to caress her shoulders, her hair, her face. He couldn't seem to stop touching her.

"Oh, Cord," Honey said with a sigh of contentment, hugging him close. She only prayed this wasn't a dream, and if it was, she never wanted to wake up.

"You'll never know how much I love you, Honey, but I'm going to spend the next fifty to sixty years showing you. Will you marry me?"

"Cord . . ." Honey began worriedly, sitting back as another thought occurred to mar her happiness. "Will my work at the airshow bother you? You said you were afraid."

Cord almost groaned in frustration. She still hadn't answered him, and the suspense was slowly driving him crazy. He couldn't really blame her for questioning him, not after the way he'd acted in the past. He knew he had a lot to make up for.

"Yes, I was afraid. I still am in many ways; I don't want to lose you. But you're good at what you do. You're a professional. I don't like seeing you in danger, and that will never change, but I'll be here from now on, making sure you're careful. It will work out, I promise."

"Are you positive you can accept my job, Cord?" she persisted. She had to be sure.

"I can accept it, Honey, because it's a part of you, just as you are a part of it. Flying, to you, is like breathing to most people—it's necessary. Though you may not believe it, flying is necessary to me as well. I'll only ask one thing of you," Cord said, more hesitant than before.

"What?"

"If we decide to have a child, I . . ." His fear was there for her to see, though he tried to hide it.

"You don't have to ask, my darling. *When* I'm pregnant, I won't do anything to jeopardize our baby," Honey said before he could finish. When she saw the tension flow out of him, she knew they'd make it. He did understand, and he loved her, all of her.

"Will you marry me, Honey?" he questioned again, looking deeply into her eyes, his hands cupping her face. He saw her answer, saw the joy and love she felt for him, and was humbled by it.

"Whenever you say, wherever you say," she replied, throwing her arms around his shoulders and hugging him, offering her lips for the loving passion of his kiss.

"You two pick the strangest places to make out," Ronnie drawled, walking down the beach to join them.

Ronnie's voice broke the moment, and Cord looked up, frowning in irritation.

"What are you doing out here at this time of the day?" Cord knew Ronnie never rose before ten, at least not voluntarily.

"Couldn't sleep. The RV was, uh, too hot."

Still holding Honey close to his chest, Cord felt the chill breeze against his arms. He arched his brow, and gave Ronnie a disbelieving look.

"What are you two doing out here?" Ronnie asked, having stopped a few feet away from them.

The sun was up, dawn had broken, and Cord could see the questions in Ronnie's eyes, and the uncertainty.

"We were talking," Cord began, "and I was trying to convince Honey to marry me."

"Well?" Ronnie asked. He looked from Cord to Honey.

Honey shifted a little in Cord's embrace so she could see Ronnie, and her smile was radiant.

"I said yes. We're getting married."

"It's about time."

"Ronnie . . ."

"Aww, shut up, Cord. This is one of the smarter things I've seen you do, other than rescuing her from the giant in the bar, and coming back for her again."

"Ronnie . . ." Honey began softly, drawing his attention back to her. Looking up at the younger man, she realized he might be feeling left out, or that he no longer belonged. She didn't want to lose him, not when he was already a member of her extended family.

"I'd like you to consider our home your home, Ronnie. You're family, you know," she said.

Honey felt Cord's breath catch and she looked up worriedly. She saw a bright flame of emotion burning in Cord's eyes, and a smile of approval on his beautiful lips.

For once, Ronnie was speechless. He and Cord exchanged a long silent look before Ronnie eventually dropped his gaze to the ground. He dug one of his ragged Reeboks into the sand.

"No one's ever wanted . . . I mean . . . I . . . You really don't have to say that, half-pint," Ronnie finally mumbled, hunching his shoulders and not bothering to look up.

"Ronnie, you *are* part of my family. You're closer to me than any friend I've ever had, more like a brother. You'll always have a place with us. Okay?" Cord said.

"Sure. I, uh, figure I might hang around a bit, then maybe head for Florida."

"Would you like some breakfast?" she offered, hoping to put Ronnie at ease. He seemed so uncomfortable, as if he didn't know what to do next.

"You bet," Ronnie said and quickly headed for the beach house without another word.

Cord and Honey stood, watching the younger man walk away.

"He's never had a real home, or anyone who loved

him. I wouldn't have asked this of you, but I'm glad all the same.''

Cord pulled Honey into his arms and kissed the side of her neck, inhaling her fresh, womanly scent. "You are a very special lady, my lady," Cord murmured.

"All yours."

"You guys coming?" Ronnie called.

Cord and Honey laughed and slowly started walking up to the house, their arms wrapped around each other.

"Are you going to mind having me around all the time?" Cord asked.

"Never," she vowed. "But what about your business, your job?"

"All I need is right here . . . You. But if you'll let me, I'd like to help manage the show."

"I'll let you do anything you want," she replied with a dreamy smile.

Cord's eyes darkened when he looked down and saw the passion firing the depths of her own. It was difficult to concentrate on what she was asking him.

"Won't you need to travel, Cord?" By this time, they had reached the steps leading up to her deck.

"No," he finally replied, having gained control of his wayward desires by remembering Ronnie was waiting for them. "I figure Ronnie can have the RV if he wants it. Dad and Antony can handle the business. If we do need to travel, we'll do it together." Cord climbed the wooden steps behind her, his hand resting intimately on the small of her back, sometimes sliding a little lower.

Honey sent a reproachful look over her shoulder, and smiled to herself when she turned back around. Cord was making plans for the future, both the immediate future and a longer range one.

Ronnie was waiting impatiently by the sliding-glass door leading into the dining room. He cleared his throat as they approached, and both Honey and Cord stopped beside him.

"Uh, I should warn you . . ."

"What?" Honey asked.

"I had a little accident in the driveway when I pulled in," Ronnie admitted, ducking his head.

"An accident?"

Cord groaned and closed his eyes.

"Well, I kind of scraped your van."

Honey glanced at Cord, then looked at the younger man, remembering the crunched fenders on the motor home.

"How much of a scrape?" she asked, almost laughing at the contrite, innocent expression Ronnie was trying so hard to convey.

"Oh, it's not bad at all," Ronnie replied.

"Well, we can take a look after breakfast," Honey promised.

A lopsided smile curved his lips, and he quickly disappeared into the beach house. When Honey moved to follow, Cord pulled her out of the doorway and back into his arms.

"I love you, Honey," he said seriously, looking down into her melting dark eyes.

"And I love you, Cord," Honey echoed, reaching up to kiss him.

"I'm glad you love me, Honey, and I want you to remember that after breakfast." Cord touched his lips to hers again, lingering to enjoy the sweetness of her mouth.

"After breakfast?" she asked. Bending back in the circle of his arms, she saw a mischievous smile curving his lips. His hazel eyes were sparkling with secrets.

"Yep. You see, the last 'little scrape' Ronnie put on a car turned it from a midsize into a compact."

SHARE THE FUN . . .
SHARE YOUR NEW-FOUND TREASURE!!

You don't want to let your new books out of your sight?
That's okay. Your friends can get their own. Order below.

No. 69 OCEAN OF DREAMS by Patricia Hagan
Is Jenny just another shipboard romance to Officer Kirk Moen?

No. 70 SUNDAY KIND OF LOVE by Lois Faye Dyer
Trace literally sweeps beautiful, ebony-haired Lily off her feet.

No. 71 ISLAND SECRETS by Darcy Rice
Chad has the power to take away Tucker's hard-earned independence.

No. 72 COMING HOME by Janis Reams Hudson
Clint always loved Lacey. Now Fate has given them another chance.

No. 73 KING'S RANSOM by Sharon Sala
Jesse was always like King's little sister. When did it all change?

No. 74 A MAN WORTH LOVING by Karen Rose Smith
Nate's middle name is 'freedom' . . . that is, until Shara comes along.

No. 75 RAINBOWS & LOVE SONGS by Catherine Sellers
Dan has more than one problem. One of them is named Kacy!

No. 76 ALWAYS ANNIE by Patty Copeland
Annie is down-to-earth and real . . . and Ted's never met anyone like her.

No. 77 FLIGHT OF THE SWAN by Lacey Dancer
Rich had decided to swear off romance for good until Christiana.

No. 78 TO LOVE A COWBOY by Laura Phillips
Dee is the dark-haired beauty that sends Nick reeling back to the past.

No. 79 SASSY LADY by Becky Barker
No matter how hard he tries, Curt can't seem to get away from Maggie.

No. 80 CRITIC'S CHOICE by Kathleen Yapp
Marlis can't do one thing right in front of her handsome houseguest.

No. 81 TUNE IN TOMORROW by Laura Michaels
Deke happily gave up life in the fast lane. Can Liz do the same?

No. 82 CALL BACK OUR YESTERDAYS by Phyllis Houseman
Michael comes to terms with his past with Laura by his side.

No. 83 ECHOES by Nancy Morse
Cathy comes home and finds love even better the second time around.

No. 84 FAIR WINDS by Helen Carras
Fate blows Eve into Vic's life and he finds he can't let her go.

No. 85 ONE SNOWY NIGHT by Ellen Moore
Randy catches Scarlett fever and he finds there's no cure.

No. 86 MAVERICK'S LADY by Linda Jenkins
Bentley considered herself worldly but she was not prepared for Reid.

No. 87 ALL THROUGH THE HOUSE by Janice Bartlett
Abigail is just doing her job but Nate blocks her every move.

No. 88 MORE THAN A MEMORY by Lois Faye Dyer
Cole and Melanie both still burn from the heat of that long ago summer.

No. 89 JUST ONE KISS by Carole Dean
Michael is Nikki's guardian angel and too handsome for his own good.

No. 90 HOLD BACK THE NIGHT by Sandra Steffen
Shane is a man with a mission and ready for anything . . . except Starr.

No. 91 FIRST MATE by Susan Macias
It only takes a minute for Mac to see that Amy isn't so little anymore.

No. 92 TO LOVE AGAIN by Dana Lynn Hites
Cord thought just one kiss would be enough. But Honey proved him wrong!
